Mark Twain
Remembers

A Novel

MARK TWAIN REMEMBERS

A NOVEL

Thomas Hauser

Barricade Books Inc.
New York, New York

Published by Barricade Books Inc.
150 Fifth Avenue
Suite 700
New York, NY 10011

ISBN: 1-56980-154-1
Library of Congress Cataloging-in-Publication Data
Hauser, Thomas,
      Mark Twain Remembers : a novel / Thomas Hauser
         p. cm.
      ISBN 1-56980-154-1 (alk. paperback)
      1. Twain, Mark, 1835-1910--Fiction. I. Title
PS3558.A759M37   1999
813'.54--dc21   99-31446
                                                              CIP

Printed in the United States of America.
10 9 8 7 6 5 4 3 2 1

FOR NANCY BRONSON,
MELODY LAWRENCE,
AND TOM HOOVER

A Note to the Reader:

This is a work of fiction. Throughout the manuscript, I have commingled Mark Twain's words and ideas with my own. I invite the reader to suspend disbelief and enjoy.

Thomas Hauser
New York, N.Y.

MARK TWAIN
REMEMBERS

A NOVEL

CHAPTER 1

I'm old now. On November thirtiethth of this year,
I shall be seventy-five years old if alive—and about the
same if dead. People never consider the age they are to
be the best one. They always put the ideal age at least
a few years older or a few years younger than they
actually are. For my own part, I now believe that life
would be infinitely happier if we could all be born at
age eighty and gradually work our way back toward
eighteen. It is now April of 1910. I believe that this
April will be my last.

During my life, I have been called everything from
a great writer to a vulgarian and a buffoon. Of the
three, I prefer being called a great writer. When I was
young, I could remember anything whether it had happened or not, and that ability fueled my writing. Now
my faculties are less reliable, and often I remember
only the latter. Still, with one exception, I have written
most of what I believe that it was ordained I should

write. Now I write one last time.

In the sport of boxing, the heavyweight champion of the world is a large colored man named Jack Johnson. Johnson mocks the entire white race by his conduct in and out of the ring. He won his crown two years ago in Australia by conquering Tommy Burns. Since then, Johnson has been unbeaten in five contests. There is awesome power in his fists. He is also a master at defensive fighting. In America, a white nation, a self-possessed colored man is now king.

It is widely assumed that only one man is capable of beating Johnson. James J. Jeffries reigned as champion from 1899 until his retirement in 1905. Jeffries has never lost a fight. He is a larger man than Johnson, and counts among his victims the likes of Tom Sharkey, James J. Corbett, and Bob Fitzsimmons. Last month, Jeffries bowed to public pressure and announced that he would wipe the smile from Jack Johnson's face. Both men are presently in training for their bout, which will take place on July 4th of this year. Their impending confrontation is the most anticipated event in the lifetime of this country. Johnson is the most hated man in America. Jeffries is the annointed savior of the white race. I am less certain than most that Jeffries will prevail.

Nor am I certain where my sympathies lie.

I shall explain.

❧ ❧ ❧ ❧ ❧

I was born in 1835. But to say simply that I was born in 1835 is a remark that states a fact without interpreting it. It is akin to giving the dimensions of a sunset by astronomical measurements and cataloging the colors by their scientific names. One doesn't see the sunset; it would have been better to paint a picture of it. So let me elaborate by saying that, when I came into the world, Andrew Jackson was President of the United States and there were soldiers still alive who had wintered with George Washington at Valley Forge. Abraham Lincoln was a store clerk in New Salem, and John Wilkes Booth had yet to be born. *The Origin of the Species* was unwritten. The average life span for a white man was thirty-eight years. Life was short for many reasons, the most prominent of them being that many children died in infancy. If a white child made it to age ten, he could anticipate living well into his forties.

The United States was composed of twenty-four states when I was born. And the country was vastly different from what it is now. The America I grew up in was a land of dreams. Its rivers and forests were unspoiled and, like the herds of buffalo that ran wild, seemingly inexhaustible. Small towns were beginning to emerge on what had once been the frontier. They might have looked like sleepy towns, but scratch the surface and you found people who were bustling with hope and excitement. Common men and common women could read. They owned the land they tilled rather than renting it from the church or some nobleman. They even had the effrontery to complain if they were not properly governed and to take hold of the government themselves.

The America I grew up in was a land where people worked by day and dreamed by night. We were idealistic, optimistic, and proud of our nation. Most of us had more hope than wealth, but our hope was well-founded because we lived in a land where people succeeded or failed based on merit. Americans were honest, straightforward, and industrious. They held to the view that a man had to earn a thing fair and square before he could enjoy it. And before them lay the richest continent in the world, ripe for the taking.

I was born in the village of Florida, Missouri; a small town in Monroe County with a population of one hundred. My parents, John Marshall Clemens and Jane Lampton Clemens, had eight children; three girls and five boys. Two of my brothers and a sister, Margaret, died before the age of ten. I was a seven-month baby, two months premature. As a child, I was often sick. Years later, when my mother was in her eighty-eighth year, I asked her if she'd been worried about me.

"The whole time," she answered.

"Afraid I wouldn't live?"

"No; afraid you would," she told me.

At birth, I was christened Samuel Langhorne Clemens. That's still my name, although most people know me now by my *nom de plume*—Mark Twain. In 1839, when I was four, my family moved to the Mississippi River town of Hannibal, Missouri. The railroad was still in its infancy, and the Mississippi was the greatest highway in America. We were poor but respectable. I suppose everybody in Hannibal was poor but did not know it, and comfortable and did know it.

My father was very grave, a man of rigid probity. He never amounted to much in business, but was kind and honorable. He laid his hand upon me in punishment only twice that I remember, and then not heavily—the first time for telling him a lie, which surprised me and showed me how unsuspicious he was, for that was not my maiden effort. My mother was a small slender woman, with a heart so large that everybody's grief and everybody's joys found welcome in it. Unlike my father, she attended church regularly, and I was raised as a Presbyterian with its traditions of damnation, fire and brimstone.

My father died when I was eleven. At that time, I left school and my formal education ended. Soon after, I stopped going to church on the theory that, if a man goes to church every Sunday, either he's a Christian or he's wasting his time. During the succeeding years, I worked at a number of jobs, but failed to impress anyone with my prowess. I was a grocery clerk for one day, but consumed so much sugar that the proprietor found it advisable to relieve me from further duty. I studied law for an entire week, but gave it up because it was tiresome. I engaged briefly in the study of blacksmithing, but wasted so much time trying to fix the bellows so it would blow itself that the master turned me adrift in disgrace. I was a bookseller's clerk, but the customers bothered me so much that I could not read with comfort. I clerked in a drug store, but my prescriptions were unlucky. And ultimately, I became a tolerable printer, albeit a slow compositor.

That brought me to the spring of 1856, when I was twenty years old. I had never been away from home, and the word "travel" had a seductive charm for me. Mainly, I wanted to be a wanderer; get away from the tedious, and journey to strange far-away locales where life was mysterious and romantic. My plan was simple. It was a six-day riverboat trip from Hannibal to St. Joseph at the edge of the Missouri frontier. From St. Joseph, one could travel the overland stage all the way to San Francisco. I vowed to travel twenty dollars worth, which would leave me somewhere in Kansas. Then I would take my leave, see what transpired, and eventually work my way to California.

I set out on my journey on the ninth day of June 1856, and arrived in St. Joseph a week later. The overland stage allowed twenty-five pounds of baggage per passenger, so my inventory was limited. Three shirts, underclothing, a spare pair of pants, two blankets, twine, a fishline and fish-hooks, a pipe, lucifer matches, smoking tobacco, and a canteen. Also, meal utensils; a frying pan, cup, knife, fork, and tin plate.

The stage company had a well-designed system.

Each two hundred and fifty miles of road was under the supervision of a manager. His job was to erect station buildings, dig wells, purchase horses, hire the station-keepers, drivers, blacksmiths, and conductors, and discharge them when circumstances warranted. There was a daily stage each way. The coaches traveled virtually twenty-four hours a day, stopping only briefly at each station to change horses and, twice a day, let on a new driver.

Our coach left St. Joseph on a sunny morning. It was a great swaying contraption drawn by six large horses, and as we pulled away from the station, I felt a great sense of freedom and exhiliration. Soon, I would be hundreds of miles from home. I would see antelope and buffalo and have all kind of adventures and maybe get hanged or scalped and write home to tell about it. The only other passenger was a sour-faced gentleman in his late-thirties, who, I came to learn, was a banker. He had the iron expression of a man who had not smiled for seven years and intended not to smile for another seven. The few words he cast in my direction had to do with common people who should know their place in society but didn't. Finally, the inclination to speak my mind overcame my diplomatic instincts, and I suggested in return that no people on earth were quite so vulgar as over-refined ones. That ended our conversation.

The coach moved quickly into Kansas, traveling a route marked by hoofprints and the trace of wheels on either side. The thick black mud of the spring thaw had dried, and dust billowed upward as we passed. The prairie was a seemingly endless expanse of coarse green grass undulating to the horizon like a motionless ocean, broken occasionally by shrubs and trees that clustered around ponds and lined the banks of streams. At night, we traveled without seeing so much as a flame to testify to another human presence. Yet the night air was scented with wild flowers, and the buzzing of insects never ceased.

Shortly before noon on the second day, we came to a small town and stopped to change drivers. Most of the buildings were made from blocks of prairie sod. The rest were sparse frame shacks, only one of which had been painted. "Ten minutes" the station-keeper told us as we disembarked. That was enough time to stretch my legs and refill my canteen with water. It was unlikely that I'd find a pleasant spot to relax, but—

Behind the station house, a voice rang out: "Hit the

nigger."

Hit the nigger. The words weren't shouted with outrage or anger. To the contrary, they sounded joyous, as though spoken by a carnival barker.

"Just half a dime. Money won't save your soul. Money is ours to purchase comfort and happiness in this life. Therefore, there is no sense in holding your money, when you can gain enjoyment from your money now. There's no need to worry. The nigger is trained. I give you my word. The nigger won't hit back."

The voice, despite the ugliness of its words, had a seductive, almost charismatic quality. I moved toward the station house, then around to the back. A small group of men, all of them white, were gathered beneath a sparse pine tree. Another man, naked above the waist with skin the color of bitter chocolate, stood off to the side. He was, at a guess, five-feet-eight-inches tall. His body was lean and his face devoid of emotion. This, apparently, was "the nigger," but it was the speaker who drew my attention. All eyes were focussed on him; and appropriately so, because I have never seen another man like him.

The speaker, too, was colored. He was a large bulky

man, more than six feet tall, weighing well over two hundred pounds with extra flesh around his middle. Despite the heat of the day, he was dressed in baggy black pants, an orange frilled shirt, black frock coat, black vest, and silk top-hat. Also black boots that looked as though they had been used to kick many a man who had been down in the dirt before him. A wilted flower was affixed to his lapel. A gold watch-chain led to a pocket in his vest. His hair, as though in defiance of the laws of gravity, rose upward toward the heavens.

"Half a dime. Five thin pennies. Hit the nigger; he won't hit back."

Drawn by the speaker's voice, I moved closer to the assemblage and our eyes met.

"Hello, son. Professor Hiram Kane's my name. You look like a man who woke up this morning and said to himself, 'I think I'll whup me a nigger.'"

I gave no answer. Almost instantaneously, Kane turned away, as though possessed of some special power that allowed him to know at a glance what others must study to understand. And with his power, he had already learned that I would not give up a half-dime for this form of entertainment.

"Of course, you can't whup the nigger with a strap or switch. You can whup the nigger with your fists. Five cents. Feels so good. This here nigger, he might move a little, raise his arms out of fear to protect himself. But it's guaranteed that this here nigger will never ever hit back."

One of the onlookers, a man in his twenties, leaned forward.

"You, sir," Kane continued, responding to the man's movement. "You appear to be a gentleman who is capable with his hands. Perhaps you would like to take advantage of this unique opportunity to demonstrate the power of a white man's fists."

The man turned toward his companion. "I reckon I never heard a colored man talk anything like this. It's part speechifying and part like he's a clown."

"Five cents. A half-dime."

"Three cents," the man in his twenties countered.

"Three cents? Three cents?" Kane bellowed, feigning insult. "Three cents? A fine upstanding gentleman such as yourself should be ashamed to—"

"Four cents," the man's companion shouted.

"Four cents. Well, four cents is more than three cents, but four cents is less than five. However, I'm a reasonable man, and I have great respect for people such as yourself who are willing to negotiate with a colored man such as myself, and I recognize that we are close to reaching an understanding. Now, four cents alone would be insufficient for the blows that you intend to land upon this unfortunate nigger. But if the two of you will pay a total of eight cents, that would be the equivalent of four cents each. And while it wouldn't be fitting and proper for the both of you to hit the nigger at the same time, I believe I could arrange for you to strike your blows one after the other for a total of eight cents."

"Seven cents total," the first man offered.

"Sir, I appreciate your kind offer. But due to the circumstances of the moment and the fact that I have certain expenses of my own in life, I must respectfully decline and insist upon eight cents."

"Eight cents," the man conceded.

Meanwhile, the smaller colored man had been standing to the side, impassive, as the negotiations progressed.

The first white man took off his shirt.

"Money first," Kane told him.

The man reached into his pocket, took out a half-dime, and handed it over. "That's my share plus a penny. We'll settle the difference later." He was anxious now to get on with the business of hurting.

The smaller colored man raised his arms in a defensive posture.

"Now," Kane chortled, "the festivities begin."

The white man moved forward. The smaller colored man stood with his feet roughly twenty inches apart, his left foot pointed forward. The white man swung; a right-handed blow directed toward the jaw. The colored man turned his head to the side and the blow sailed harmlessly by. The white man swung again, this time a blow to the body, and the colored man dropped an elbow to his side for protection. Another blow aimed at the head struck the colored man's raised hand.

Kane's voice sounded above the fray, as noticeable as a false note in music. "Ah, yes; the glory of our times. Only a half-dime. Hit the nigger."

I stood watching, part fascinated and part revulsed.

The voice of the station-keeper interrupted my thoughts. "Last call! Stagecoach is leaving."

I turned to go, but not before casting one last glance over my shoulder toward Hiram Kane. At the moment, he was acting the buffoon. But beneath his veneer, I thought I saw an extraordinary meanness about him.

Then it was back on the stagecoach again. There were occasional hills, ridges and valleys, but mostly we traveled across a great level prairie. Wild turkeys and prairie hens were abundant, sharing the land with wolves, snakes and badgers. The daytime heat was tempered by prairie breezes, and the nights were pleasantly mild. By the third day, though, the landscape was less green and the perennial springs less plentiful. The wild strawberry plants that marked our earlier passage were no longer in evidence, and my twenty dollars worth of travel was just about exhausted.

It was then that we came to a comfortable-looking town in northwestern Kansas near the Nebraska border. Its main steeet was three blocks long, with several brick buildings interspersed between white frame stores. There was a sidewalk made of boards that were loose and inclined to rattle when walked upon. Several of the stores had awnings in front, and all of them offered hitching posts for horses. A few narrow lanes extended off the main street, but not very far before turning to wheat.

Something in the town sang to me; I really can't tell you why. It seemed like a good place to stop and rest for however long it was meant to be. So not knowing what lay ahead, I said goodbye to my banker traveling companion and left the stagecoach to meet my destiny.

In the main, the events of life are small events. They seem large only when we are close to them. But the occurrences of the days that followed still loom large in my mind. They changed me. They altered what I believe. Much of what goes on around me today is blurred. But even now, more than fifty years later, the days I spent in this small Kansas town are still sharp and vivid in my memory.

Everything that I am about to recount for you is the truth, precisely as it happened to me.

CHAPTER 2

The town where I found myself was surrounded by small farms. Dreams were plentiful. Land was cheap. People were building homes and tilling soil that had never been turned before. They were concerned with the nuances of daily life; not with what was going on in faraway regions or the halls of Congress. But whether they liked it or not, Kansas was becoming part of a larger national drama.

Europeans first set foot in Kansas in 1541, when a Spanish expedition crossed its plains in search of wealthier lands. It was sold to the United States in 1803 as part of the Louisiana Purchase, and for the next half-century remained an Indian land, serving as a way-station for emigrants to Utah and California. Then, in 1854, its status changed.

Years earlier, Congress had enacted The Missouri Compromise. Under that law, Missouri was admitted to the Union as a "slave state" and Maine as a "free state." Thus, an even balance between pro- and anti-slavery forces was maintained. It was also written into law as part of The Missouri Compromise that slavery would be prohibited forever in all territory ceded by France to the United States that lay north of 36° 30' except for Missouri. Thus, slavery was ruled out in the territories that would ultimately become Kansas, Nebraska, Iowa, Colorado, and the Dakotas.

In 1850, another compromise was forged between pro- and anti-slavery forces. California entered the Union as a free state. Texas (which had been admitted in 1845 as a "slave state") gave up its claims to New Mexico and the Utah territory. It was agreed that, whenever New Mexico and Utah were admitted to the Union, their status with regard to slavery would be determined by their respective state constitutions. And a severe Fugitive Slave Act was passed. Under this law, special commissioners were appointed and given juris-diction concurrent with the federal courts to order the return of fugitive slaves from one state to another with the assistance of United States marshalls.

Then, in 1854, Congress passed the Kansas-Nebraska Act. The act's primary architect was Stephen Douglas of Illinois—the foremost advocate on Capitol

Hill for America's railroad interests. Before railroads could be built in Kansas and Nebraska, those lands had to be settled and territorial governments organized. The Kansas-Nebraska Act expressly repealed that portion of The Missouri Compromise that precluded slavery in Kansas and Nebraska. Now, Congress decreed, all questions pertaining to slavery in those two territories would be left to their respective territorial legislatures.

After passage of the Kansas-Nebraska Act, settlers began moving into Kansas and Nebraska in great number. Nebraska was clearly within the orbit of "free states." But Kansas was adjacent to the slave state of Missouri, and attracted settlers from both north and south. In March 1855, a territorial legislature was elected in Kansas. Shortly before the election, thousands of Missourians crossed over the border to establish temporary residence in Kansas. They voted and then returned home to Missouri. The result of this "stacked" election was a pro-slavery legislature. Immediately thereafter, the new legislature enacted a series of laws that prescribed the death penalty for anyone who aided a fugitive slave and two years at hard labor for anyone who so much as questioned the legality of slavery in Kansas. In late 1855, "free-soil" Kansans met in Topeka to draw up their own constitution, and in January 1856, they elected a rival legislature. Meanwhile, both sides were arming themselves in ever-increasing numbers.

In May 1856, a group of pro-slavery Kansans raided the town of Lawrence, Kansas, in search of free-soil leaders who had been indicted for treason by the pro-slavery legislature. They burned homes, destroyed a free-soil printing press, and killed two men in "The Sack of Lawrence." In retaliation, John Brown of Osawatomie gathered six followers, rode into the pro-slavery community of Pottawatomie Creek, and hacked five men to death. A "holy war" was brewing, and hundreds died in the scattered conflicts that followed.

In the midst of all this, I arrived in what was becoming known as "Bleeding Kansas."

My own views on slavery were formed in the Mississippi River town of Hannibal, Missouri. Missouri was a slave state, and I will be honest with you in saying that in my youth I had no aversion to slavery. I now believe that it is a crime against God for men and women to be owned by another. But growing up, I was not aware that there was anything wrong about it. No one had spoken against slavery in my presence. The local newspaper said nothing against it. The local pulpit taught us that God appproved of slavery, that it was a holy thing, and that doubters need only look in the Bible if they wished to settle their mind. Then the texts were read aloud to us to make the matter sure. And if the slaves themselves had any aversion to slavery, they were wise and said nothing.

My father owned slaves during my youth. On occasion, he would cuff our slave boy, Lewis, for awkwardness or a trifling blunder. Often, I summered on the farm of my uncle, John Quarles, who owned in excess of thirty slaves. But slavery in Hannibal was mild domestic slavery, not the brutal plantation kind. Overt cruelties were rare. To separate and sell the members of a slave family to different masters was frowned upon and not often done, except in settling estates. Once, when I was ten years old, I saw a man fling a lump of iron ore in anger at a slave for performing a chore poorly. The ore struck the slave's skull. He fell and was dead in an hour. Nobody in the village approved of the man's deed, although no one said much about it either. The incident caused me a certain amount of concern, but was soon forgotten. And I remember walking with one of my uncle's slaves; a large woman named Della. I was perhaps eight years old at the time. We were in the woods, and I asked her if she had any children.

"Hush, child," Della told me. "You don't want to know nuthin' 'bout that."

Remembering that moment, even today, I remember that Della's eyes were sad. Still, whenever I hear people say that slavery made everyone who lived in its midst hard-hearted, I protest. Slavery was a horrible institution that stupefied everybody's humanity as regarded the slave. But the people I grew up with in Hannibal were as loving and kind as those anywhere else in the world. Some might think me foolish and ignorant, maybe even cruel, for those sentiments. But to arrive at a just estimate of a man's character, one must judge him by the standards of his time.

ᘐ ᘐ ᘐ ᘐ ᘐ

As I mentioned before, the town I was drawn to in Kansas lay in the northwest corner of the territory. Its citizens were "free soilers," farmers for the most part, who were untouched by the bloody turmoil in regions to the south. I watched the stagecoach that had been my home for several days move toward the horizon. Then, feeling the late afternoon sun on my face, I took a longer look at my surroundings.

I was standing halfway down the town's main street. On one side, I saw a general store, bank, and jail. The largest building was a two-story wood structure opposite the bank. Painted brown with red and gold trim, it bore a sign that read "The Silver Slipper." I assumed it was a saloon. A young man about my age rode by on a gray horse, glanced toward me, and kept riding. Then I saw a boy of about sixteen standing by the jail. He was short and fat, poorly dressed, with coarse brown hair and a face that looked as though he'd been thrown from a horse and landed flat on his nose. He appeared to be doing nothing more than resting on one foot to relieve the other, and perhaps half-dozing.

I walked toward him, and extended my hand.

"My name is Sam Clemens."

The boy looked up, a bit startled, and I realized he had a knife in his hand.

"My name is Pete. I've been carvin' my name here." He touched his knife to the hitching post beside him. "P and E is what I've done so far. I can't read too good, but I know how to write 'Pete.'" At which point, he went back to carving, laboriously as it were, and it was hard to tell whether his pace was occasioned by the demands of carving or the slowness of his thoughts.

"Pete, where can I find a room around here?"

"Well, I reckon that depends."

There was no further response, and I decided that it would do no harm to inquire a bit further.

"When a man passes through town, where might he spend the night?"

Pete looked up from his work, and I had the sense that it was too much for him to carve and think at the same time.

"Well, Miss Lurleen over at The Silver Slipper has the best rooms in town. I don't go there none, because my mother tells me to stay away from the saloon. There's drinkin' and gamblin'. And my mother, she tells me, early to bed and early to rise will make me healthy, wealthy, and wise."

Whatever Pete's sleeping habits, I had the sense that his mother would be disappointed if her expectations were high, particularly with regard to wisdom. If Pete wasn't the village idiot, probably he was close to it. But then he showed a helpful side.

"I reckon I can walk you to the saloon, even if I

don't go inside."

We crossed the street. Pete stopped on the sidewalk, and from there I went forward alone through the saloon's swinging door. It took a moment for my eyes to adjust to the dim interior light. Then I became more comfortable and began to survey my environs.

I was standing in a large room with a finished hardwood floor. A bar with several bottles of whiskey behind it dominated the wall to my left. A poker table surrounded by chairs stood near the wall opposite the bar. There was a second table, a half-dozen more chairs; and a staircase leading to a balcony. The balcony, I later learned, led to five small rooms with beds on the second floor.

The saloon was close to empty. Only the bartender and a man who looked to be a year or two older than I was were inside. I approached the bartender and asked him if there was a room available for the night.

"Miss Lurleen has the final say," he told me. "But my guess is, you'll be all right."

"This Miss Lurleen sounds like an influential lady."

"Miss Lurleen owns The Silver Slipper. Right now, she's upstairs resting, but I can give you a room subject to her approval."

The room rate was fifty cents a night. That was more than I wanted to spend, given the fact that honest labor in Kansas paid an average of twenty dollars a month. But the saloon had a comfortable look and seemed like a good place to start. Besides, if I stayed in town for any length of time, I could find less expensive lodging.

The bartender directed me to a room on the second floor. It was small but clean with a slanting ceiling. A tin wash basin lay on the floor next to a large pail of water and piece of yellow soap. I set my belongings beside the bed, and went back downstairs to the bar. A third man, also in his twenties, had joined the others. He told me his name was Cowhand Bob. I didn't believe someone could really be named Cowhand Bob, so I asked if that was his true full name. He said, no, that his parents had named him Robert W. Hopkins, but that he kind of liked "Cowhand Bob."

The four of us talked for a while. Then the bartender mentioned that Marshall Bassett would soon be passing by. The marshall walked along main street every afternoon at five o'clock. He was a reliable man, and anyone who chose to do so could set a timepiece by him. I was curious to see what a Kansas lawman looked like. And having been confined to a stagecoach for the better part of three days, I wanted to stretch my legs, so I went outside to walk a bit and wait for Marshall Bassett.

The sun had dropped closer to the horizon, although this being June there would be several more hours of light. The street was empty, except for a horse and wagon tied to a hitching post outside the general store. Pete was nowhere in sight.

Then I saw a vision the likes of which I had never seen before. A young woman perhaps eighteen years old.

She was the most beautiful girl I'd ever seen.

I will leave that thought in a paragraph by itself. It cannot be made too conspicuous.

She walked out of the general store . . . unhitched her horse . . . climbed onto her wagon . . . and rode by.

As she passed, I thought she looked at me with approval.

But perhaps that was my imagination.

CHAPTER 3

At precisely five o'clock, a tall powerfully built man in his mid-thirties walked out onto the town's main street and looked around. He was wearing coarse pants, a cotton shirt, leather vest, and broad-brimmed hat. Before I ever saw his badge, I knew he was the marshall. He had a look about him that said, I'm the law in this town; I'm a fair man, but don't trifle with me. The way he carried himself spoke of integrity and strength, but it was also the look of a man whose dictates could be ignored only at great peril.

I walked over and introduced myself. Marshall Bassett asked what my business was in town. I told him. He didn't seem particularly impressed, but he wasn't particularly bothered by it either. Then he asked if I'd like to take a walk. "Folks here are friendly people," he said as we ambled down the street. "The only thing they don't like is when someone comes along who thinks he's better than they are."

As Marshall Bassett and I passed the saloon, Cowhand Bob came out and joined us. He recounted for me how, several years before, the marshall had singlehandedly tracked down a pair of killer desperados, shooting one through the heart and setting in motion the wheels of justice that led the other to the gallows. It was the stuff of legends and dime-store novels. And I had the sense that the marshall was a rich man; not in monetary terms, but because he seemed to have everything in life that he wanted.

After our walk, I went back to the saloon. There were a dozen men at the bar; some with side-whiskers and mustaches, none with beards. Everyone seemed in good spirits. I ordered a whiskey, and the bartender pointed toward a woman standing at the far end of the room.

"That's Miss Lurleen," he told me.

Mindful that Miss Lurleen had the power to remove me from my room and deposit me on the street, I went over to make her acquaintance. She was of medium height with brown hair; perhaps thirty years old, which at the time seemed quite mature to me. Also, and of greater interest, Miss Lurleen was wearing a rather elegant dress that exposed the northern slope of her breasts and offered considerable insight into the deep valley that lay between them. Or phrased differently, she was as large on top as those women who were put on canvas by that European painter, Reubens, but on the bottom she was more slender.

Miss Lurleen seemed to approve of me. I had my drink at the bar, and then went upstairs to my room. There was a candle by the bed for light, but the sun had yet to set. Only a fool shows his money when he travels, and most of mine was in the lining of my coat. After taking off my clothes, I unstitched a small portion of the seam and extracted a five-dollar gold piece to see me through the next week. That chore complete, I sewed the lining back up and went to sleep before it was dark.

Over the next few days, I got to know most of the people in town. Marshall Bassett had been right. They were friendly, and when a stranger was pleasant, they responded in kind. There was a small cattle ranch nearby. The ranch-hands were rough uneducated men, but seemed honest and faithful to their promises. The farmers outnumbered the cowhands and were a quieter breed. However, I sensed that, this summer at least, their farms were not fully supporting them. Instead, they were struggling to support their farms.

I ate most of my meals at the saloon, where the common fare was biscuits, bread, eggs, coffee, bacon, cheese and vegetables. In addition to the bartender, Miss Lurleen employed another man who assisted around the place and was a serviceable piano player. And there were two women, Mona and Judith, who lived in rooms on the second floor.

Mona was tall with a hard look about her. She smiled from time to time, but it never seemed real. She had the look of a woman who, even when fully dressed, didn't look fully dressed. Judith was almost as tall as Mona; a bit awkward, maybe even clumsy, but outgoing and friendly like Miss Lurleen. Mona and Judith helped keep the saloon running. After I'd been in town a while, I heard a story about how Mona had once danced with the top of her dress pulled down while the piano player played some kind of French song. But it was only a story. No one knew anyone who, when pressed, could honestly say that he'd been there to see it happen.

Other than Mona and Judith—and Miss Lurleen, of course—I never saw a woman in The Silver Slipper. I will acknowledge, however, that fairly soon I began

having thoughts about Miss Lurleen. She was an
earthy woman, but one with a certain stately grace. She
had a hearty laugh, as though she enjoyed her life, and
part of me was in awe of her.

Meanwhile, after three days in town, I had yet to
find a job. I had reasonably good skills as a printer, but
there was no local newspaper. I was tolerable at counting large sums of money, but the bank wasn't about to
put its assets in the hands of a stranger; and besides, it
already had a teller. Not being able to ride a horse with
any proficiency, I was an unlikely candidate for work
as a cowhand; and regardless of ability, I had no desire
to work with cows. Nor did I want to be a farmer.

Thus, my financial situation was very much in
doubt as I walked along main street on my fourth day
in town. It was a Saturday morning and I was
engrossed in thought, when—

"Come one, come all! Wager a half-dime and win
two bits! Just step in with the nigger—"

I stopped and sought out the familiar voice that was
alluring and repelling at the same time.

"Wager a half-dime and win two bits; a return on
your money that's fivefold."

I moved toward the sound, down the street, behind

the general store. Eight or nine people had gathered around a large colored man.

"Professor Hiram Kane's my name, and I'm here with an offer and an opportunity for each and every one of you. You see this nigger over here; this scrawny pitiful nigger. Well, each of you can walk away from here with two bits more in your pocket than you came with. All you got to do is wager a half-dime and then stand on your feet for two minutes against this nigger. Now the nigger is a clean fighter. He won't be allowed to hold or kick. I won't permit it. You, of course, may do as you please. All you're required to do is stand on your feet without falling to the ground for two short minutes, and two bits will be yours."

"What's in the cloth around the nigger's hands?" one of the onlookers demanded.

"This nigger has weak hands," Kane answered. "The cloth will protect his hands from damage, and also protects gentlemen such as yourself from being cut should the nigger strike a blow against your person." There was a pause, but only a momentary one, before Kane continued in the cadence of a carnival barker. "You may, of course, examine the cloth."

"How do we know you got the two bits?" This time,

the questioner was a farmer who had come to town for supplies and heard Kane's voice behind the general store.

"Sir, I assure you. I may be colored, but I am a man of my word." Kane reached into his pocket, drew out several coins, and held them aloft for the crowd. "And I am a man of means."

The number of onlookers had grown to a dozen.

"How do we know when the two minutes are up?"

"In my pocket, kind sir, I have a watch. We will count together as the seconds pass by."

The farmer shrugged. "I reckon I'll try."

"Excellent; we have a match."

The farmer gave Kane a half-dime. Then he and the smaller colored man stepped forward and faced each other, awaiting a signal from Kane that would begin their confrontation. The farmer was the larger of the two combatants. He raised his hands and positioned them defensively.

"Time," Kane shouted.

The two men warily eyed each other and began a strange dance without actually striking any blows. As I'd seen several days before, the colored man's feet were spread twenty inches apart, left foot in front pointed toward his adversary. His fists were chest high; his right hand held in reserve.

"One minute and forty seconds," Kane shouted. "We raise de wheat; dey gib us de chaff. We bake de bread; dey gib us de crust."

Both men were posturing defensively. Occasionally, the farmer feigned a blow, but his forays seemed unintended to do damage. Rather, he was warning his colored opponent to keep his distance until two minutes had passed.

"One minute and twenty seconds. We sift de meal; dey gib us the husk. We peel de meat; dey gib us de skin. And dat's de way dey take us in. Poor nigger, we can't get over dat."

The farmer continued to stand flatfooted, moving his fists in menacing fashion but not striking any blows. The colored man's left hand flashed forward, striking the farmer on the cheek and snapping his head back. In retaliation, the farmer threw a righthand punch, but the colored man moved his head to the side and avoided it.

"One minute. Dey say dat's good enough for a nigger. Walk over; walk over. Your butter and de fat."

The combatants came together in a sort of embrace,

and the colored man appeared to whisper something in the farmer's ear. The farmer was standing with his back to me in such a way that the colored man was largely obscured from view.

And then the farmer was lying in the dust, moaning, clutching his stomach. "The man is down," Kane shouted. "Praise Jesus; what a surprise!"

I was unimpressed. The entire happening had the look of fraud.

After a rest, the farmer picked himself up and rejoined the crowd. He seemed a bit pale, but none the worse for wear. Kane was shouting again, "Professor Hiram Kane's my name, and each of you can walk away from here with two bits more in your pocket than you have in your pocket now. All you got to do is wager a half-dime and stand on your feet for two minutes against this nigger."

I wanted the two bits. That's what was going through my mind. I had no job. I was in a strange town. And while there was sufficient coinage in the lining of my coat to see me through the immediate future, I preferred not to dip into capital any more than was required.

"I'll try," I said.

It was foolhardy on my part; or rash at best. I was never a fighter; at least not with my fists. At my healthiest, I was of slight physique; small-boned with narrow shoulders; five-feet-eight-inches tall; never more than a hundred fifty pounds. My only previous confrontation of note had occurred when I was eight years old. A bully of ten, who was bigger and stronger than I was, had decided to taunt and shove me, so I picked up a board and whacked him over the head with it. The bully ran away and, the next day, confronted me with a board of his own. I persuaded him that, since he was bigger and stronger than I was, he didn't need a board to give me a licking. So he put his board down, intent upon beating me up in the traditional manner, at which point I grabbed his board and whacked him over the head with it.

I gave Kane my half-dime.

The colored man and I moved forward to face each other. We were about the same height and weight, but his body seemed different from mine. Suddenly, I realized that this was the first time in my life that I had faced a colored man who was at liberty to strike me, and a tremor of fear swept through me.

"Time," Kane shouted.

I raised my arms in the manner most likely to protect my face and began moving in a semi-circle. The colored man seemed to be stalking, but in an almost halfhearted fashion.

"One minute and fifty seconds."

I did my best to blot out Kane's voice and focus on the task at hand.

"One minute and forty seconds."

One of the colored man's hands flashed toward me faster than I could follow, and slapped against my chin. It was more of a tap than a punch with bad intentions, but the impact shook me nonetheless.

"One minute and thirty seconds .... One minute and twenty seconds ...."

I threw a punch with my right hand as a warning to my adversary to keep his distance. But it came nowhere near his head, and I felt both foolish and awkward.

"One minute."

Better to act defensively. In sixty seconds, the two bits would be mine.

"Fifty seconds."

Never in reality or in my imagination had time passed so slowly. My arms were beginning to feel heavy. The colored man drew closer to me.

"Forty seconds."

I threw a punch. The colored man blocked it with his arms, and pressed his body against mine. "Fall down, sir."

I ignored him and stepped back, but the colored man moved forward again and stayed pressed against me.

"Fall down, sir," he repeated in well-enunciated English. "I don't want to hurt you."

"Thirty seconds," Kane shouted.

And then I felt a searing pain, the likes of which I'd never felt before. It began in the pit of my stomach, as though a two-by-four had been rammed through me. It spread quickly to my legs which went numb, and to my lungs which gasped futilely for air. I lay on the ground in a fetal position, unable to move, oblivious to every-thing but pain.

Then, gradually, the pain eased. I rose unsteadily to my feet. The townfolk were looking at me. Mona had come out from the saloon during the fight, and she too was among them. I was embarrassed, and didn't know what to say. Finally, I mumbled, "It's harder than it looks." Then, humiliated, I turned away and began to walk toward the sanctuary of my room with Kane's voice sounding behind me: "Come one, come all. Stay on your feet for two minutes. Wager a half-dime and win two-bits. Look at this poor pitiful nigger."

 ❧ ❧ ❧ ❧ ❧

Miss Lurleen was in the saloon when I returned from the debacle. I figured that, sooner or later, she'd hear what had happened, so I might as well tell her first. My version wasn't pretty, but it was the truth.

"You men are all the same," Miss Lurleen said when I'd finished. But she said it with a look that seemed sympathetic.

I went to my room and lay down on my bed. Actually, I was in pretty fair shape, considering the fact that, several minutes earlier, it had felt as though I'd never breathe again. I rested for a while, and then went downstairs back out onto the street. The activity was normal for a Saturday afternoon. Kane's voice was nowhere to be heard. Contemplating the experience just past, I circled behind the general store. The crowd was gone. A solitary figure was sitting on the ground, with a half-loaf of bread in his hand. I drew closer, the man looked up, and I realized it was my conqueror.

I nodded in recognition. For a moment, he seemed to shrink back, as though fearing my humiliation had been so great that I'd come to even the score between us with a gun. Then he saw that I meant him no harm, and went back to eating his bread.

"Hello," I said. And I sat down beside him. His forearms were strong. There was a scar above his left eye. Several of his upper teeth were missing.

"My name is Sam Clemens."

Perhaps he intended to answer; maybe not. I never found out.

"Get away from my nigger," a voice ordered.

I looked up and saw Hiram Kane coming toward me.

"That man is a slave, formerly the property of Mr. Josiah Clark, now deceased. He is presently my property. I own that nigger."

It wasn't unheard-of in the decades before the Civil War for one colored person to own another. Most of those situations involved family relationships and a way around state laws that prohibited slaves from being freed. But there were also entrepreneurial Negro planters in South Carolina, Louisiana, and Virginia who owned as many as one hundred indentured servants.

Still, it wasn't what I'd expected.

"Get away from my nigger." Kane's voice was rising, and I felt the beginnings of fear. "The law gives me a right to defend my property. When a man tries to steal another man's nigger—"

Then I saw the marshall coming toward us, drawn by the commotion and intent that calm should prevail.

"What's the problem?" Marshall Bassett demanded.

Kane's tone changed from anger to deference. "Marshall, I'm thankful you're here."

"What's the problem?" the marshall repeated.

"Sir, I am a free Negro. I was formerly the property of Mr. Josiah Clark, now tragically deceased. However, I am presently free and a propertied slave-owner. This nigger sitting at my feet is my slave. All the official papers are in order. I fully appreciate that I'm in your town, and I don't mean to cause no trouble. I'm a law-abiding colored man, who's grateful for the opportunity that this great country has given me. However, this other gentlemen was interfering with my property."

The marshall looked at me; then at Kane and the man who was purportedly Kane's chattel. "Does this man own you?"

"Yes sir," the smaller man answered. "The man that

owned me before passed title to him. I don't know everything 'bout how it came about, but I know he's got somethin' on paper."

The marshall shrugged. "Let's go," he told me. "This is none of your business."

"But—"

"Sam, I said we're going. You might not like it, but these folks have the same right to be here as anyone else, yourself included. The law is the law, and in my town I enforce it."

So I walked off with the marshall, leaving Kane and his property alone behind the general store. The rest of the afternoon passed without incident. I wrote a letter to my mother and brothers and sisters in Missouri, knowing it would take weeks to be delivered. I took a long walk and went to the creek to bathe.

Late in the day, I returned to the saloon. It was more crowded than usual, this being Saturday. Mona was standing at the bar, flirting with a man I'd never seen before. He smelled of sagebrush; she of perfume. The piano player was at work, and words ran through my mind to match the tune he was playing:

Buffalo gals won't you come out tonight,
Come out tonight, come out tonight.

Buffalo gals won't you come out tonight,
And dance by the light of the moon.

Then, from the corner where a poker game was in progress, I heard a laugh. And without looking, I knew it was Hiram Kane.

There was an empty chair. I walked over and addressed the players in general. "Mind if I join you?"

Kane took it upon himself to answer. "How good a player are you?"

"Not bad."

"Son; you can lose a large amount of money when you gamble with me."

"That means I can win a lot too."

Kane laughed—actually, it was more of a cackle— and gestured toward the empty chair. "You wouldn't cheat a nigger, would you?"

"I don't believe in cheating any man."

"That's mighty fine. I'm the same way."

There were four other players in the game. Two had familiar faces; the other two were strangers. One of the latter was serving as banker, and it was his responsibility to exchange chips for money. There was no central bank in the United States in 1856. Each state issued its own paper currency, but coins were what people trusted. The federal government issued hard currency made of gold, silver, and copper. Coins from most other nations were also generally accepted. Metal content was what mattered.

"Hard currency only," one of the players said.

I reached into my pocket for the loose coins I had left, and exchanged them for a pile of chips. Kane was sitting directly to my right, which meant I'd have the advantage of betting after him. The other players introduced themselves, and I did the same. Then the game resumed. Five card stud.

Kane won the first hand with a pair of kings that bettered the jacks the player to my left was holding. After a two-hand interval, he won twice more, including once on his own deal.

"That's quite a streak of luck you're riding," I offered.

"Poker isn't a game of luck, Mr. Clemens. It's a game of skill. And a game of lying."

"Lying, Mr. Kane?"

"That's right. Lying. With one's eyes, with one's smile, and mostly with one's bets. Sometimes a man has aces below, but when he bets, he bides his time.

And sometimes he bets his entire stake with nothing but a ten high."

Kane tossed his ante into the pot, the last of us to do so, and the game resumed.

"Of course, Mr. Clemens, there's a line between lying and cheating. It's not cheating for me to notice that, every time you get a good card facing down, you frown like you got something bad. And it's not cheating for me to watch what goes on in your eyes. But suppose someone was wearing spectacles, Mr. Clemens. Would it be cheating for me to look for the reflection of cards in the glass that covers his eyes? Or suppose I positioned myself so I could see your cards reflecting in that window to your right?"

As the game went on, I made an effort to measure everyone at the table. In poker, any player can walk away with your money, so it's important not to take anyone lightly. Still, Kane was the adversary who interested me the most. At a guess, he was close to forty; well-fed but with a look that said he'd always want more. He seemed unencumbered by honesty; a man who would always snub fair dealing in favor of artistic villainy. His heart was most likely only a pump. There was no love in him that I could discern.

Generally, in poker, it's sound judgment to play your hand boldly for more than it's worth. Most of the time, nobody will challenge and you will find yourself raking in chips. Also, a good poker player must be selfish. Kane played with a combination of recklessness and calculation. His attitude said that nothing in the world mattered at all except his own needs. And he was a good player. He'd look at his hole card when it was dealt, and never look at it again. His eyes were fixed on everyone else; learning our mannerisms, studying our moves.

Poker took hold in the United States in the late 1700s. It began in New Orleans, and spread to the territories in the person of riverboat gamblers. I grew up in Hannibal, Missouri, on the banks of the Mississippi River. I knew quite a few things about poker. Still do.

Hiram Kane was cheating.

The game went on .... Shuffle .... Cut .... Ante .... Deal.... Highest face card bets first .... Call .... Fold.... Raise .... More cards.

After an hour, Kane was the big winner. One of the strangers dropped out of the game, and was soon replaced by another. I was still biding my time, a little ahead of where I'd started.

"You're better than I thought," Kane told me. "When I saw you at that stagecoach station, I never figured you for a poker player."

His remark was designed to intimidate me, and it was not without effect. If Hiram Kane remembered me from that brief interlude earlier in the week when I'd seen him orchestrate "hit the nigger"—

Pay attention to the game, I told myself. But the urge to respond was too great to resist. "Back where I come from, people own slaves, but we don't beat them for a carnival act."

"Oh no, Mr. Clemens. Back where you come from, people do things that are much worse."

"I don't recall seeing coloreds on display in Missouri and being told I can hit them for five cents."

Kane's face took on a hard look. "Dat's right, massuh. I's so happy you neber beat me wid yo fiss. Corse my back is welted like a washbord. But dem whippins done me good, massah. Dey done stopped me from thievin' an all dat." Kane laughed. "Spare me, Mr. Clemens. The weakest virtue of all is a virtue that has never been tested in the fire."

"Deal the cards," one of the other players said.

We played four more hands. Kane won one. But

clearly, I'd gotten under his skin. Now he was playing against me instead of against everyone at the table.

Shuffle .... Cut .... Ante .... Deal ....

Over the course of the next few hands, Kane moved the position of his cards to the left so they were within casual touching distance of mine. That gave him certain opportunities. Of course, the opportunities were mutual.

I got lucky and won two hands in a row; the second when I called Kane's bluff.

"Never waste a lie, Mr. Kane," I needled. "You might need it in the future."

"I'm not worried," Kane responded. "I've got more lies where that one came from."

The player to my left won handsomely with a flush.

Then Kane won a hand when the rest of us folded.

"That's right, Mr. Clemens. The way to get along with me is to let me have my way."

"With one unfortunate slave, at least, it seems you always have your way."

"It bothers you, doesn't it, Mr. Clemens; that a man of my color is entitled to hold property. But I am one of God's creations, so you must treat me with dignity and respect."

"Is that how you treat your slave?"

"Seeking to equalize what God has made unequal would be terribly wrong. I'm a businessman, Mr. Clemens. Your high ideals might be wonderful, but I doubt there's any money in them. Besides, the Bible teaches us to respect slavery. 'Both thy bondsmen and thy bondmaids, which thou shalt have, shall be of the heathen that are about you. Of them shall ye buy bondsmen and bondmaids.' Chapter twenty-five, Leviticus."

It was Kane's deal again, and he distributed the cards; one down and one up for each of us. I had an ace in the hole. On the board, Kane's king was high.

"Two bits," he said.

I matched his bet. Two of the other players did the same, and the other two folded.

Kane dealt another round. An ace for me; a queen for himself. "Ace bets," he said.

I threw in a dollar.

Kane and the man to his right matched me. The fourth player folded.

Three of us left. Three more cards were dealt. We bet again. The player to Kane's right tossed in his cards.

The final round was dealt. A jack for me and a second queen for Kane. That meant I had an ace in the hole, with an ace, jack, seven and four showing. Kane had a king, a nine, and a pair of queens on the board, with one more card hidden.

The mathematics of the situation were simple. With my ace in the hole, I had a pair of aces. Kane had at least a pair of queens, and his hole card could bring him victory. He'd started the hand with a king in the hole. I knew that, because I'd seen him cheating. He'd dealt the king to himself at the start from the bottom of the deck.

The whole hand was a set up. My pair of aces against Kane's two pair. All he had to do now was keep the hook in me and slowly reel me in.

"Now it gets interesting," Kane said. And he pushed a pile of chips toward the center of the table.

"How much is that?"

"It doesn't matter, Mr. Clemens. I've got two queens. You can't beat me."

"Maybe I've got an ace in the hole."

"I doubt it."

In truth, Kane knew I had the second ace, because he'd deliberately dealt it to me. But he also knew he had me beat. I was working with five cards, and he'd had fifty-two to play with. He was sitting pretty.

Or so he thought. Between the third and fourth round of bets, I'd managed to change his hole card.

"How much was your last bet?" I asked, pointing toward the table.

"Do you really want me to count it, Mr. Clemens?"

"Mr. Kane, why don't we make this simple."

Either I'd done this right, or I was in big trouble. With a flourish, I pushed all of my chips—maybe twelve dollars worth--toward the center of the table.

"That's very brave of you, Mr. Clemens. Now I suppose we have to count your chips to see what I need to call you."

"That won't be necessary, Mr. Kane. Take your chips out, and I'll play you for your nigger."

Kane looked at me scornfully.

"The nigger's worth a thousand dollars. You got a thousand dollars to back that up?"

"No, Mr. Kane. All my money is in front of you, right in the center of the table."

"I'm afraid that's not good enough."

"Then let me sweeten the pot."

I reached into my pocket, took out my watch, and

tossed it beside the chips.

I was counting on Kane's greed. He wasn't a man to let a watch slide by when he could win it on a sure bet. His eyes narrowed and his face took on what seemed like a particularly hard look.

"Well, Mr. Kane?"

His eyes never leaving mine, Kane reached into his vest, took out a folded paper, and threw it onto the table.

"Mr. Clemens, I'd say I feel sorry for you, but wealth comes from the misfortune of others. I have no pity for another man's sorrow."

Then he turned his hole card over.

And showed no reaction. That was what amazed me most. Hiram Kane looked down at the card, which had been a king of hearts at the beginning of the deal and was now a worthless seven. Something had gone horribly wrong from his point of view. He knew he'd been had, and yet he showed absolutely no reaction.

"Mr. Kane; I think I have you beat. A pair of aces beats a pair of queens."

"Very well, Mr. Clemens. The nigger is yours. I believe our game of cards is over."

There remained the formality of the transfer. Kane had both a deed of property and a letter of safe passage from the now-deceased Josiah Clark. Kane asked to keep the letter. Most slave states required "free Negroes" to carry their freedom papers at all times, and it was also advisable to carry a "letter of protection." The deed of property was sufficient for my purposes, so I told Kane he could keep the letter.

Miss Lurleen suggested that I ask the marshall to witness the signing of the deed transfer. If a question of title arose in the future, his word would carry considerable weight. One of the farmers agreed to serve as the second witness. Cowhand Bob went and got the Marshall, after which the deed was presented to Kane and myself for signature. There was an awkward moment when it appeared as though Kane was unwilling to sign. Then I realized it was a matter of his not knowing how to write.

Kane marked his "X" in the appropriate spot. I signed beneath him, and the witnesses' attestations were put in place.

"All right," the marshall said. "Let's get this business over with." He looked at Kane. "Where's your bondsman?"

"I'll take you to him," Kane said.

We walked to a clearing by the creek about a mile from the center of town. I was glad the marshall was with us. I wouldn't have felt safe without him. Kane was silent as we began our journey, but before long he was talking.

"You know, Mr. Clemens, I killed a man once. I was a slave. I was playing cards with some other slaves, and this other slave was cheating. I had to defend my honor or lose my credibility, so I stuck him with my knife."

"Nobody's accusing anybody of cheating," the marshall cautioned. "We're all honest."

We came to the clearing. The colored man I'd seen with Kane earlier in the day was lying on the ground beside a fire. If he was concerned by the presence of strangers, he kept his fear well-hidden.

Kane gestured toward me and said simply, "You belong to him."

That was all. "You belong to him." And without a word, the man stood up, not having a clue as to how his life might change. I could be planning to sell him down river, or be intent on beating him to avenge my humiliation of that morning. I could be a gentle angel or the most sadistic malfeasant on earth.

The marshall was in no mood to tarry. "Let's go," he instructed.

The colored man leaned over and picked up a small sack.

"Goodbye, Mr. Kane," the marshall said in a way that indicated Kane wasn't to follow. "Now that your business in town is complete, I'm sure you'll be moving on."

"Goodbye, Marshall. And goodbye, Mr. Clemens. I'm certain we'll meet again."

As Kane spoke, his eyes were full of malice. He was a man with many layers, and I knew I never wanted to explore whatever lay deepest within him.

The marshall began to walk. My slave and I went with him.

"My slave." I ran the words through the recesses of my mind. They had a ring that was both empowering and foreboding.

"What's your name?" I asked.

"Bones."

"How old are you."

"'Bout thirty-three."

"How long have you been with Kane?"

"Two years, sir, since the master died. Before that,

we was both owned."

It didn't take long to return to town, but as we walked I began to learn the history of my chattel. Bones and Kane had been the property of a South Carolina planter named Josiah Clark. Clark had come into possession of Bones when the latter was eight years old, and had trained him as a house servant. Then, recognizing that Bones had unusual physical gifts, Clark taught him to fight and matched him against other slaves for amusement and occasional profit. Fights between slaves were generally ugly. Combatants were awarded prizes when they won, and were frequently punished when they lost. Occasionally, when two particularly skilled opponents met in the ring, the winner would be given his freedom. But such contests were generally avoided because of a master's desire to protect his investment in his property.

"Mr. Clark was a good master," Bones told me as we walked. "He never forced me when I didn't want to fight. And he listened to my troubles like I was white."

Josiah Clark fell gravely ill in 1854. As death approached, he expressed the desire to free Bones and a half-dozen other slaves. But South Carolina had a strict law regarding manumission that provided a slave could be freed only by special legislative enactment. That presented a problem, but Clark saw a way around it. Hiram Kane was his head driver. At Clark's urging, the legislature passed a private bill enabling Clark to grant Kane his freedom. Then Clark passed title to Bones and five other slaves to Kane with instructions that he deliver them to freedom.

It never happened. After Josiah Clark's death, Hiram Kane was a slaveholder six times over. He sold five of his charges to a slave trader. Bones was the sixth.

"He had my papers," Bones explained as the marshall led us back toward town. "He said someday he'd give them to me, but first I had to do some fights."

"How many?"

"The number kept changin'."

"What did he pay you for the fights?"

"It wasn't about payin'. It was about him someday givin' me my freedom. Sometimes he'd get angry at me and threaten to sell me down river. But Mr. Kane wasn't a bad master. He never whupped me. He fed me good. Sometimes the fights was hard, but mostly they was carnival acts that kept me ready for real fightin'."

We arrived back at the center of town, and stopped

on the sidewalk in front of the bank. "I don't mean to interfere," the marshall told me, "but right now you're responsible for this man and where he spends the night." And just in case I'd missed the point, Marshall Bassett nodded toward The Silver Slipper. "In case you're wondering, there's never been a colored that slept in there, and things aren't about to change tonight."

"What do you suggest?"

"Let him sleep out back, alone. Then in the morning, if he's still here, you can figure out what to do with him."

Which sounded as though the marshall didn't take my status as a property owner very seriously. And that made sense, because I wasn't sure how seriously to take it either.

The marshall left. I looked at Bones and gestured for him to sit on the sidewalk. He did, and I did the same. Bones had the look of a man who didn't know what was coming next. At least Kane was the devil he'd known. I might be far worse.

"You're a free man," I said.

Bones sat silent, as though he hadn't heard, or didn't believe, the words I'd just uttered.

"You're a free man," I said again. "I'll sign the papers over to you in the morning."

"Why you be doin' that?"

"I didn't like the way Kane was treating you. No one has the right to treat another man like that."

Bones sat still. And let out his breath.

I wanted to shout. You're free! Get excited!

"What do I do now?" Bones said.

And as dumb and insensitive as I might have been, I understood.

"Don't got no money. Don't got no home. Takes time for a man to prepare for freedom."

So I sat there and asked myself whether Bones and I might not both be better off if I'd never sat down to play poker that afternoon. I'd played because I wanted the money. Then pride or whatever had gotten in the way, and now I was sitting next to a slave I owned who might not even want to be free.

"Bones, do you want your freedom?"

"Yes, sir."

"My name isn't sir. Call me Sam."

"Yes, sir; Mister Sam."

"Not Mister Sam. Sam."

"Yes, sir; Sam."

The wheels in my head were turning.

"Bones; I've got an offer for you. Suppose we do some fights together?"

There was no response.

"Listen to me. You know how to fight, and I know about business. You fight, and I'll handle the money. Everything gets divided even between us. And any time you want, you quit. All you do is say so, and you walk away a free man."

"What you talkin' bout?"

"Look, I'm making this offer fair and square. You don't know me, and right now there's no reason for you to trust me. Probably, you think all I'm doing is looking to take advantage of you. But there's an easy way for you to judge me. Anytime you want, you leave."

For the first time in my presence, Bones smiled.

"Is it a deal?" I pressed.

He nodded. But something was missing. So I stuck out my hand.

Bones stared and slowly extended his hand toward mine.

And then, at age twenty, for the first time in my life, I shook hands with a colored person.

CHAPTER 4

After Bones and I shook hands on our understanding, I went to my room in the saloon for the night. The next morning, I woke up half-expecting him to be gone. But he was where he said he'd be, in a field about a hundred yards behind the general store.

Meanwhile, the money I'd won playing poker had improved my finances but also given me the reputation of a pretty savvy player, if not a downright cheat. That meant it was unadvisable for me to play cards for a while, and no other guaranteed income was in sight. Thus, a change in living accommodations seemed in order.

I made some inquiries and learned of a widow named Alma Peaks, who lived just outside of town with her son. The widow had a bed to spare, and our agreement was simple. She would provide lodging and two meals a day in exchange for fifty cents a week and a few manual chores. Bones was allowed to sleep in her

THOMAS HAUSER

barn.

It would be accurate but misleading to say that Widow Peaks lived on a small farm. It wasn't really a farm; just a dozen chickens, a tired old horse, and a plot where some vegetables were growing. Her house was made of logs chinked with clay set over a crude wooden floor. The privy wasn't a real outhouse so much as a hole in the ground surrounded by boards.

The widow was on the stout side, hard of hearing and slow of foot. Also, she was a truly horrible cook. Her formula for meals consisted of taking whatever odds and ends were on hand, striking at them with a knife, adding a few hairs, and seasoning the mess with dish water to suit her taste. I would have preferred her concoctions without the hair, but obviously she felt differently about the matter since hair was always included. After several days of this torture, I found a promising nook in a nearby creek and began to fish for dinner. However, conscience compelled me to share what I caught with the widow, thus leaving me with good food furnished by God that, by the time it reached my plate, tasted as though it had been cooked by the devil.

The widow's son was none other than Pete, who I'd met my first day in town. Confirming my initial impression, Pete was painfully simple-minded. The contents of his skull could have been exchanged for those of an apple pie, and only the pie would have been the worse for it. Regardless of the advice his mother gave him—"early to bed, early to rise"—Pete spent much of each day sleeping. He was incapable of performing any but the most basic chore. And he ran to the privy more than anyone I've known in my life, but only after announcing the reason for his departure each time he left.

The chores that Bones and I performed were simple. Splitting wood, cleaning out the barn, mending the chicken coop. On occasion, Pete joined us but he was more of a burden than a help.

"Gotta fix the coop," he announced one day when he took it upon himself to aid us. "Dumb chickens. Gotta fix the coop."

"Pete; if you'd like to help, hand me the wire-cutter."

"Sure thing, Sam. I'll get the wire-cutter."

After which eternity came and went without any sign of the wire-cutter.

"Pete!"

"I know; I know. Gotta get the wire-cutter, but first

I have to go wee-wee."

Like Pete, Bones was uneducated. But unlike Pete, he showed considerable natural intelligence. He'd been born prematurely and was a thin sickly child; hence the name "Bones." Then his parents died, he was sold to a new owner, and his life had proceeded from there.

Bones was superstitious and believed in spirits. "The ghosts that wander don't mean no harm," he told me one night as darkness fell. "They wander 'cause they'se lonely and lookin' for someone." He viewed rainbows as omens, which caused me to reflect on how much we've lost by prying into nature's origins. And he was the first person I'd known who refused to eat meat, fish, or fowl. "I eat food the way God gave it to me, without killin' of no kind," he explained.

One time, I debated the point. "It's the way of the world," I told him. "Look at the jungle; look at the prairie. Animals kill and eat each other."

"I don't see cows killin' no other animal. I don't see chickens eatin' other livin' things."

The chores we performed for Widow Peaks took up relatively little time, which left us free for wandering. The farm was within walking distance of town, and I visited The Silver Slipper fairly often. There was a stretch of three days with rain, which made things a bit gloomy. But as Cowhand Bob observed philosophically, "If every day was a sunshine day, we'd have an awful bad drought."

It was during one of those rainy afternoons that I began planning for Bones's first fight. In the week we'd been together, I'd come to realize that his skills went far beyond the ordinary. Every day, he went through a series of exercises designed to strengthen the muscles in his stomach, arms, and neck. He stretched into a hundred different positions, lifted stones as weights, and ran to increase his stamina. I'd seen slaves with great strength before, but none as quick and graceful as Bones. He had special physical gifts, and moved differently from the people I'd known. Also, I realized that the carnival events Kane subjected him to had served a positive purpose as well. They'd enabled him to keep his reflexes sharp and stay in fighting condition.

The first fistic business venture I planned was relatively easy to orchestrate. July fourth was coming, and the entire community would be getting together for a holiday social. That meant there'd be a ready audience, and the challenge I faced was how to take advantage of it. I figured Bones could fight two fights. Each fight would be for three rounds. A round would end after three minutes or when a man got knocked down, whichever happened first. At the end of each fight, whoever knocked the other man down more often would be declared the winner.

As for how to make money, it was essential that people pay to watch the fights. But what would keep them from watching for free? I could erect a tent, but that would be expensive and it would be dark inside. We could travel to some out-of-the-way place, but I doubted that many people would follow. Finally, I decided to operate on an honor system. Each person who watched a fight would be asked to contribute a half-dime. Twenty percent of the proceeds would, as a matter of course, go to Bones and myself. The other eighty percent would be awarded to the winner of each fight. It took a few days to choose the opponents. I was new in town and wanted to proceed slowly in order to avoid a mistake. But by July fourth, everything was in place.

The social was held in a clearing behind the church, and just about everyone from the community was there. My experience with these things has been that women worry about what to wear, while men are concerned with what they eat. Neither side was disappointed. Most of the women came with sunbonnets. A few were wearing gingham dresses; the rest chose calico. And the tables were piled high with food. Fried chicken, roast pig, rabbit, biscuits, wheat bread, corn pone, corn on the cob, succotash, stringbeans, butterbeans, tomatoes, sweet potatoes, buttermilk, watermelon, apple pie, peach pie, pumpkin pie.

And it was a day of celebration, because the Fourth of July is truly a time to brag about Old Glory. You see, real civilization began with the American Revolution. I'm not talking about mythology now, and that nonsense about George Washington saying, "Father, I cannot tell a lie; I threw a cherry tree across the Potomac River." I'm talking about America giving Lady Liberty a home. When we took her in, she'd been a vagrant for six thousand years. And not only did we give her safe haven; we made her respectable on a permanent basis.

Most of the people I knew from town were at the social, along with quite a few others whom I'd never seen before. Bones's first fight began at noon. The opponent was a large colored man, who worked on a nearby farm. Before the contest, Bones wrapped a long narrow piece of cloth around his wrist, looped it around his thumb twice and around the back of his hand several times before tucking it in at the wrist. Then he closed his fist completely to protect his knuckles and give himself a flat striking surface.

About thirty people had gathered around the fighting area that I'd cordoned off with rope. To my delight, all but one paid a half-dime. There were a few side bets, and the action began.

The large colored man came out cautiously, moving his upper body from side to side. Bones seemed to glide forward, his weight balanced on the balls of his feet. Then his left hand shot forward and at the same time he advanced his left shoulder, thereby extending his reach. The blow landed flush on his opponent's nose, and the large colored man flinched .... Bones jabbed again, successfully scoring against his intended target .... The large colored man threw a righthanded punch, and Bones moved his head to the side to avoid it.... Bones faked a jab.... Then, bending his left arm at the elbow with his palm facing down, he turned his body at the waist and rocketed his fist into the pit of his opponent's stomach. A loud groan accompanied by the involuntary compression of air escaped the large colored man's lips.

He sagged. And Bones hit him with a righthanded punch that was almost a caress to put him down.

After the allotted minute of rest, the large colored man returned to the center of the ring, but it wasn't an equal fight. Again and again, Bones struck quickly followed by a defensive retreat. While being aggressive, he was always ready to evade his opponent's blows. On those rare occasions when the larger man scored, Bones absorbed the punch with no outward sign of distress. I was watching a craftsman at work. The difference between brute strength and science was clear.

The second round ended when Bones sent his opponent to the ground with another hard blow to the body. Then, in the final stanza, he fought with restraint, allowing the larger colored man to finish with dignity. Overall, the crowd was pleased. There had been some blood from the opponent's nose. No one had been badly hurt. They were ready for more, and willing to pay for more. Only now, the number of paying onlookers had grown to about forty.

The second opponent was white. That had troubled me some when I set things up, because I wasn't sure how the crowd would react to watching Bones strike one of their own. His name was Jason Trapp, and he was a cowpuncher on a ranch several miles from town.

Jason came out firing away and, to his great dismay, Bones fired back. People who aren't used to cuts are often upset by the sight of blood; particularly when the blood is their own. After forty seconds of battle, Trapp was bleeding from the nose and lying on the ground. In round two, his face continued to register each of Bones's blows. If God had given Mr. Trapp two heads, we might have seen more combat. But since the Deity gave him only one, and Bones was about to knock it off, wisdom dictated that he not come to scratch for the third round.

I was enormously pleased with it all. I'd made some money and had some fun. The social still had several hours to run, and I was at liberty to enjoy the rest of the afternoon. To celebrate, I put some tobacco in my pipe, lit it with a lucifer match, and began to stroll around.

The first person I chatted with was Horace Fuller, the town doctor, who I reckon was as successful in curing and killing as most of his brethren. Doc Fuller confided in me that business was slow because folks in the county were distressingly healthy that summer.

Then I visited with Ezra Moore, who claimed to be

celebrating his eightieth birthday. Mr. Moore was the town's oldest resident and possibly the oldest person in Kansas. He'd been born on July 4, 1776, or so he claimed. I never saw his birth certificate, but he looked eighty and there were lots of wrinkles on his face to indicate where the smiles had been.

Next, I said hello to Pete, who was sitting at a table with a pile of food in front of him.

"I'm eatin', Sam."

"I can see that, Pete."

"This is my fourth piece of pig. And soon as I finish, I'm goin' back for more."

I figured that five helpings of pork might make Pete sick, but probably wouldn't kill him.

"Sam; let me ask you something. Right when I got here, I sat on a spider. Is that good luck or bad luck?"

"Pete, I'm not a hundred percent sure; but I think it's bad luck for the spider."

After that, I stopped to listen to a fiddler and a banjo player.

Mona was flirting with a cowhand.

Judith was dancing with some children.

Miss Lurleen and Marshall Bassett were sitting off to the side, talking with each other. There seemed a sort of intimacy between them, so I wandered over to Cowhand Bob and asked if Miss Lurleen was the marshall's woman.

"I don't think so," Cowhand Bob told me. "But the marshall kind of looks after her."

And then, suddenly, I heard bells ringing. The kind of bells that ring from churches on clear sunny days when all is right with the world; except these bells were ringing in my heart. The most beautiful girl I'd ever seen, the same girl who'd been in front of the general store my first day in town, was walking toward the gathering. She was slender and graceful with long auburn hair and a look of purity about her. Her face radiated innocence, with all of its girlish airs. Her features were fine and her complexion was fair, as though she were made of angel clay. Yet as my heart soared, I feared she was unapproachable for I was wholly in awe of her.

She stopped at the edge of the gathering, as though looking for a friend. Then I heard Pete shouting.

"Nell! Nell!"

She seemed to hear him, but didn't acknowledge his call.

"Nell! Nell! Hello, Nell!"

Perhaps to quiet his voice, she turned and walked toward him.

"Nell; there's pig and chicken and corn and pie. You can have some off my plate if you want."

"Why, thank you, Pete. That's very kind. But I want you to enjoy it all."

In every man's life there are opportune moments; and if he fails to take advantage of them, he will mourn their passing forever. Exercising only modest care not to trample anyone, I crossed the clearing as quickly as possible and positioned myself at Pete's side.

"Hello, Pete."

He ignored me.

"Pete; aren't you going to introduce me to your friend?"

Maybe he would have; maybe not. But before he could answer, the vision looked at me and smiled.

"I don't believe I've had the pleasure, sir."

"My name is Sam Clemens."

"And I'm Nell Trimble."

She wasn't pretty, she was beautiful. With green eyes that shone like emeralds.

"How long have you been in town, Mr. Clemens?"

"About two weeks .... You can call me Sam."

And then there was an awkward silent moment, accompanied by the fear that everything to be said between us had been spoken.

Nell smiled again. "Whereabouts are you from, Sam?"

"Missouri."

"Well then; you've come a ways. Do you plan on staying?"

"I just might, ma'am."

"Hey, Nell," Pete interrupted. "This mornin', there was ants killin' each other. I saw them over at the farm."

Nell shrugged ever so slightly. "Pete," she said gently, "why don't you talk with some of the other folks, so Sam and I can visit a while."

If Pete's face showed resentment, I didn't see it. I was deep into Nell's eyes.

"All right, Nell. I'll get some pie. Goodbye, Nell."

And then, as if by magic, I was walking with Nell Trimble.

"Pete's really very sweet," she told me. "And he'd do anything for me; I'm sure."

The next few hours passed more quickly than any afternoon I've known. Nell and I laughed a lot. I remember the adornments of ribbon-knots she wore, and a moment when she tilted her head back to watch a jayhawk in the sky. The bird soared higher, and higher still, but its flight would never have been able to match the euphoria I was feeling. It was a very special time. I was young and confident, knowledgeable and strong; and it was a joy to be alive.

At the end of the day, I walked Nell to her wagon.

"I do hope you'll visit sometime."

"I will," I promised.

"Thank you, Sam."

Then Bones and I went back to the farm. He had a few bruises on his arms, but nothing that was cause for concern. Both of us had eaten a lot during the day, so neither of us was hungry. We sat outside Widow Peaks's barn and reflected on the day just done.

"Most folks pull their arm back before they punch," Bones told me. "They think it gives them strength on the blow. But when a man pulls his arm back, I see the punch comin' before it's throwed."

We talked about the surprise of big strong men, who'd never tried to hit a skilled defensive fighter before. Also, the reaction of men who were hit for the first time by someone properly trained in punching. By now, I realized how much damage Bones could have inflicted on me when I'd tried to win two bits from Hiram Kane. He could have cracked my ribs and smashed my nose in my moment of folly.

"I want to thank you," I said.

"What for?"

"Not hurting me when I was foolish enough to fight with you behind the general store."

Bones smiled the smile of a man who hadn't been thanked for much of anything in his life. Then, as he looked on, I emptied my pockets. Thirty people had paid to watch the first fight; forty-two to watch the second. That meant we'd taken in a total of three dollars and sixty cents.

I divided the money into two piles; a dollar and eighty cents in each.

"This is yours," I said, and I pushed one of the piles toward him.

Bones sat motionless.

"Take it. It's yours."

"For me?"

"For you. I said I'd give you half. Remember? We shook hands on it."

And I was aware of a strange incongruity. For much

of the day, I'd basked in the glory of another man's triumph. I had built up my own self-esteem by virtue of my association with a colored.

But more important than anything else, I had met Nell.

That night, I felt very good about myself. As I lay in bed, an old nursery rhyme kept going through my mind:

> *Lavender blue and rosemary green*
> *When I am king, you shall be queen.*

Then, eventually, I closed my eyes and fell into that mysterious void called sleep.

In the morning, I woke up and went down to the creek. Bones was bathing and didn't hear my approach. His back was turned toward me.

It was a warm sunny day, like the day before. I sat down beneath a tree at the edge of the water. Two turtles, neither one bigger than the face of a pocketwatch, moved slowly toward me. A black-and-green water snake glided by. A large bullfrog croaked at the interloper, and jumped off a log in the opposite direction.

Bones turned and, still unaware of my presence,

began to step from the water.

I stared.

Horror .... Anger .... Revulsion ....

There was a scar, the likes of which I'd never seen before.

"How did it happen?"

Bones stood silent.

"What did they do to you?"

More silence ....

And then Bones told me his story.

CHAPTER 5

There are times when words are inadequate. They realize nothing and vivify nothing, unless one has suffered in his own life the thing which another person is trying to describe. Nonetheless, I shall try to recount Bones's story. And I will do so as dispassionately as possible, because the facts and their horror speak for themselves.

Slavery is as old as history. The Egyptians of Biblical times forced the Jews into slavery. The glory of Rome was built upon slaves. During the Crusades, Christians and Moslems enslaved one another. The tribes of Africa have a long history of conquest and enslavement.

A half-century before Christopher Columbus journeyed to the New World, the Portuguese began the importation of African slaves to Europe. France, Spain, Holland, and England followed in kind. As profits rose, treaties were negotiated and the slave trade became more widespread. By the mid-1700s, the British West Indies alone had imported almost two million African slaves, and neighboring regions were engaged in similar commerce.

In the early years of the thirteen colonies' existence, white indentured servants outnumbered African slaves. In 1715, there were fewer than 60,000 slaves on the American mainland, and by 1804, all of the northern states had abolished slavery. However, in the American South, servitude was burgeoning. Hot summers, long growing seasons, rich soil, and navigable waterways led to an agricultural economy. That in turn, created a demand for cheap unskilled labor to cultivate "the five great staples"—cotton, tobacco, rice, hemp, and sugar. The invention of the cotton gin in 1793 further increased the demand for slave labor. In 1807, Congress banned the importation of slaves. But by then, there were one million slaves in the United States, and a domestic slave trade was flourishing.

Slavery in the South was first and foremost a practical labor system; a means of earning the greatest return for a landowner on his investment. Slaves were articles of property, classified under law less as people than as chattel. Often, they were treated as domestic animals. In response to the question, "Who are you?" a slave was taught to give his name followed by the name of his master. They were denied the simplest forms of human identity, such as knowledge of date of birth and a hereditary name. Many slaves knew nothing about things as basic as the months of the year. They measured time in relation to the number of planting seasons and harvests that passed.

The ideal slave was docile and meek. He had no mind or opinions of his own. Throughout the South, it was a crime punishable by imprisonment to teach a slave to read and write. Unfettered knowledge was considered dangerous. A slave was to think only as his master thought, speak only as his master dictated, and do only what his master approved of. In sum, a slave was to know nothing but the will of his owner.

The relationship between master and slave undermined the development of honor at both ends. It codified a form of misery, insult, and oppression that sapped the spirit from all who were part of the system, and created a society based on degradation. Yet over time, slavery became the bedrock of life in the South. Through the thoughts and traditions of generation after generation, it grew into a complex economic and social structure that was inextricably intertwined with Southern culture. There was no way to eliminate slavery without casting into turmoil the entire society that was built upon it.

And what crime did the slaves commit so that bondage was thrust upon them?

The moral rationale for slavery rested on the belief that Africans were innately inferior to white Americans, unfit for freedom, and unable to care for themselves. Thus, slavery was the only existence for which they were suited. Africans were happier and better provided for in slavery than would be the case if they were free. A great wrong would be done to them if they were removed from bondage and placed upon a higher, more demanding plane. Indeed, the worst calamity that could befall a slave would be to lose his freedom from responsibility and be forced to deal with the tribulations that white people faced every day. Slavery had elevated the African from the depths of barbarism to a degree of civilization, utility, and contentment that would have been unachievable by other means.

And one thing more. Slavery was God's will.

The Church came to the fore and propped up slavery with platitudes to fortify the evil. It preached patience in the face of the unendurable, humility under insult, endless self-sacrifice, and non-resistance to oppression. It sanctioned the belief that a man could be both a good Christian and the owner of slaves, and that God had entrusted the care of the colored race to slave-holders. It taught the slave to know no law higher than the will of the master; that offenses against the master were offenses against God; that come Judgment Day, the slave would face eternal salvation or eternal damnation, and a slave's loyalty and devotion to his master would be the standard by which he was judged by God. Thus did the Church enslave the weak, separate families, and wash the world in blood, so that Christian nations might prosper.

Big Henry was born in 1800, the property of Sherrod Gray. Slaves were economically valuable if they served one of two ends: labor or reproduction. Gray made a handsome profit by breeding and raising slaves. He bought slave women for the purpose of bearing children, and paid stud fees to the owners of strong healthy males who impregnated the women. Big Henry was the product of such a union.

For the first six years of his life, Henry [he was not

known as "Big Henry" until he went to the fields] was constantly at his mother's side. Then he was sold.

I say that matter-of-factly. Then he was sold. If you prefer drama, I can imagine Henry's mother learning that she and her son were about to be torn apart and would never see each other again. I can imagine her falling to her knees and pleading with Sherrod Gray to spare her son in words only a mother could command. Having been thus appealed to, Gray would have disengaged himself from this clinging woman with a kick and blows, so that the groan of her physical suffering mingled with the sobs of her heart. And I can imagine her shrieking like one gone mad, struggling to free herself from the bondsmen who held her down, as her son disappeared from view in a caravan of slaves.

The caravan would have made its way to market; in this case, a slave trading center in New Orleans. After Henry joined them, the slaves marched on foot, fueled by the stingiest of rations for twelve days. Chains joined their manacled wrists, and they were linked six feet apart by a single chain that led from collar to collar down the line. They slept in their irons every night, bundled together like swine. The trader in charge rode a large black horse and carried a whip with a heavy lash knotted at the end. With this whip, he cut the back of any slave who moved too slowly or tottered from weariness and pain. The slaves made no sound as they walked, other than the awful clank of their chains. Their faces grew tinged with a coating of dirt, not unlike the dust that accumulates on furniture in unoccupied homes. Looking closely at the dust, one might have seen the track of tears.

In New Orleans, the slaves were prepared for auction. Older bondsmen were shaved of their whiskers, and gray hairs were plucked from their heads. Where the gray was too widespread, dye was applied with a blacking brush. Before the auction, each slave was subjected to inspection in the manner of a cow or horse. Prospective buyers examined their teeth, squeezed their muscles, and ordered them to walk. Then the slaves were put up for bid. The highest prices were paid for prime field hands and pretty young women. Henry was six, but he was large for his age and looked to be eight. That presented a quandary for the trader. He could say Henry was eight, which would increase his value in that prospective buyers could look forward to his laboring in the fields shortly. Or he could tell the truth—that Henry was six—and promote his value as an uncommonly large physical specimen. The trader decided that, since no one would believe what he said anyway, he would let Henry's presence speak for itself. Henry was sold for four hundred dollars. His purchaser was 24-year-old Gabriel Crow, who had recently inherited his father's fortune and was a member of the planter aristocracy in Mississippi.

To put things in perspective, three-quarters of all whites in the antebellum South were poor and owned no slaves. Most of the rest were small farmers, who often worked in the fields beside their bondsmen. However, in Mississippi, the greatest cotton-growing region in the world, more than fifty percent of white families owned slaves. And in several Mississippi counties, slaves outnumbered whites by a ratio of ten to one.

The plantation that Gabriel Crow inherited from his father lay amidst primeval trees on two thousand acres of rich soil in Mississippi's delta region. It had barns, stables, a storehouse, greenhouse, henhouse, dairy, cooper shop, and slave quarters. Also, a huge white mansion with a grand portico and eight columns that was home to the Crow family. To the slaves, the great white house must have looked like the building that

God himself lived in.

Crow inherited so many bondsmen from his father—
five hundred and forty, to be precise—that he couldn't
recognize most of them. For the most part, his chattel
reproduced themselves, but a stretch of bad fortune
had come his way. A dozen slaves had died of cholera,
and an entry in his diary revealed, "The slave Hattie
had a child born dead last night; this in addition to the
two that were stillborn last month. My luck this year
is uncommonly poor." Thus, his decision to purchase
Henry.

It must be difficult to handle as simple property a
human being with feelings and emotions. But slavery
was as much a part of Gabriel Crow's life as the blood
that coursed through his veins. He had been so born
and so educated, and his spirit was full of ancestral rot
that had been brought down by inheritance from a long
procession of hearts, each heart having done its share
to poison the stream. Indeed, his own father had taught
him that God created Africans specifically to labor for
white men: "The white race could never raise cotton or
sugar through its own manual labor. In our swamps
and under our hot sun, we would die, but the colored
slave flourishes. Some men are born with saddles on

their backs, while others are booted and spurred to ride them."

Crow viewed his slaveholdings as immune from reproach, and understood his duty to his caste. The Lord had watched over him since infancy, and given no sign of disapproval. Indeed, the Bible commanded him to rule his servants, as it commanded all servants to "Be obedient to your masters according to the flesh." Thus, Gabriel Crow considered himself God's overseer on earth, and he taught his slaves accordingly: "When you are lazy and neglectful of my business, when you steal or waste my goods, when you are stubborn or sullen in my sight; these are sins against God himself who has set me above you. You were sent into this world for a wise and good purpose, and you must accept your life as you find it. You must do your duty without repining and serve me as you would serve God. Those of you who live like this will enjoy a noble and beautiful reward in the hereafter."

The slaves on Gabriel Crow's plantation struggled to succeed; meaning by success that they lived and did not die. Woe to the bondsman who had an insolent look, walked too tall, or spoke with a tone of defiance. Proper slave behavior was meant to embody burden without honor. Lack of spirit, not the weight of one's load, was the accepted cause for stooped shoulders.

Crow himself administered the plantation, which was a complex agricultural organization. He oversaw all finance and marketing, and periodically inspected slave conditions. His most gifted bondsmen served as livestock specialists, blacksmiths, mechanics, carpenters, and stone masons. Others found a niche as butlers, maids, and cooks. These house servants were the aristocrats of the slave class, and received more and better amenities than their field counterparts. The vast majority of Crow's slaves cultivated cotton. Bondsmen who were too old for hard labor performed other tasks. Old women nursed the sick and cared for slave children. Old men cleaned stables and fed animals until the day was done.

Crow had three overseers who ruled the day-to-day life of his slaves. The head overseer was a career practitioner, employed on a year-to-year contract that provided for lodging, meals, a personal servant, and seventy dollars a month. He'd held the job for many years, and Crow was fortunate to have him. The assistant overseers were less skilled, and there was frequent turnover among them. One was fired because he treated the slaves too leniently. Then his successor was let go because he was a brutal drunk, unfit to manage a team of mules, let alone more valuable chattel.

As was the case on most plantations, Crow's slaves were exempt from work on Sundays, except as punishment or when work was voluntarily undertaken for token pay. Christmas was a holiday, accompanied by small gifts such as tobacco for the men and handkerchiefs for the women. In good years, Crow did not require his slaves to work at all during the week that stretched from Christmas to New Year's Day.

In return for their labor, Crow's bondsmen received food, clothing, shelter, and medical care. These items were essential for maintenance, since slaves, like animals, could not be expected to work unless given the necessities that nature required for them. The weekly food ration for each slave was a peck of corn and four pounds of salt pork with a few supplementary items added. Male slaves were given two cotton shirts and two pairs of pants each spring; and two cotton shirts, a pair of pants, a wool jacket, and a pair of shoes each autumn. Slave women were given three dresses that reached slightly below the knee annually. The children wore long shirts and nothing else. A wool blanket was provided every third year. The average maintenance cost for each of Crow's slaves was nineteen dollars per annum.

Crow was pleased with his purchase of Henry. Many of the slaves on his father's plantation had been native Africans. That meant they'd been resistant to captivity and difficult to train. But slaves who'd been born into bondage and knew nothing beyond servitude were malleable. Because Henry was large for his age, he was sent at age six to carry water in the fields. By age eight, he was removing stones from in front of plows. At ten, he was performing adult chores.

Year after year, the same story unfolded. Days began before sunrise, when a bell rang to wake Crow's bondsmen. At good daylight, a second bell sounded, indicating that it was time to go to the fields. The slaves were divided into crews, with each slave laboring within his group until its assigned tasks were done. To spur the slaves to maximum production, several bondsmen were chosen as drivers. The head driver was exempt from labor, while the other drivers set a pace by working beside their fellow slaves. In March and April, the slaves opened furrows in the ground, sowed cotton seeds, and covered them by hand. From May through August, the cotton was bared and surrounding weeds were pulled. Then, beginning in September and lasting for four months, the cotton was picked, ginned, and pressed. January and February were a time for repairs and preparing the ground for another year. In March, the cycle began anew.

By age fourteen, Big Henry, as he had become known, could do the work of two men. By sixteen, he stood six-and-a-half feet tall, an almost unheard-of height. His shoulders were awe-inspiring. His biceps had the feel of iron. He was the most imposing physical specimen that Gabriel Crow, or anyone else on the plantation, had ever seen. And he was strikingly handsome.

But he refused to breed . . . . It was as though he accepted his own indentured state, but was unwilling to take part in the creation of another life that would be exposed to so much humiliation and suffering.

And Gabriel Crow was beside himself, because he could only begin to imagine the wealth in Big Henry's seed.

Then, at age seventeen, Big Henry began to look fondly on a slave girl named Lilah. She was fourteen years old; a mulatto and one of the most beautiful woman that anyone on the plantation had ever seen. Normally, beauty was a curse for a slave, because it led to all manner of predatory sexual conduct. But Garbriel Crow decreed upon penalty of death that no one but Big Henry was to lie with Lilah.

Still nothing happened .... Until one day, at the age of eighteen, Big Henry told Gabriel Crow that he wanted to marry Lilah.

Big Henry's request presented a quandary for his master. Slaves were property and could not enter into contracts, so slave marriages were not recognized under Mississippi law. Some masters allowed their slaves to "marry" because they thought it encouraged stability on the plantation. But Crow was not among them. And in any event, slave marriages were most often performed by a bride and groom simply jumping over a broom in the presence of their master. Big Henry wanted more than that. He wanted a Christian wedding.

For almost a fortnight, Crow wrestled with implications inherent in Big Henry's desire. As a young man and a good white Christian, he had once entertained doubts about the propriety of baptizing slaves for fear that baptism might entitle them to freedom. However, eventually he had come to the view that encouraging slaves to be Christian both saved souls and served as a useful instrument of control. In principle, he supposed, the marriage of Big Henry and Lilah would be no different from a baptism. And he wanted to own their children.

Big Henry and Lilah were married on Christmas Day 1818. Thereafter, Big Henry lived as he had lived before. He and nine other slaves shared a windowless hovel. They slept on straw, covered by blankets of lesser quality than those used to shelter their master's horses. The roof leaked and the dirt floor, which was level with the ground outside, turned to mud when it rained. Only now, when Big Henry slept, Lilah slept beside him.

Gabriel Crow could hardly conceal his glee at the prospect of owning Big Henry's offspring. But two years passed; and then two more. And Lilah was still without child. Big Henry lay with her often, doing what might be expected of him and more. However, Lilah remained barren until finally, in 1823 at age twenty, her body began to swell.

Children brought no increase in responsibility for slave women on Crow's plantation. In fact, during pregnancy, chores were lessened to facilitate the birth of a healthy child. Lilah was especially pampered, and the birth of her issue—Big Henry's progeny—was more eagerly awaited than the birth of a champion thoroughbred's foal.

Two months before the expected date of birth, Big Henry began having visions in his sleep that death would strike his child. Each night, he awoke in a sweat, groveled in the dirt, and prayed to God to save his innocent blood. Lilah suffered uncommon pain during her pregnancy. Five weeks before the child was due, it was born.

A son .... Small and sickly.... Big Henry stood over the babe at birth, wiped the tears from his own massive cheeks, and caressed his wife and child.

"Once again, fate has been unkind to me," Gabriel Crow wrote in his diary. "The infant is a runt. I fear it will die."

Because of the child's emaciated body, Crow named him Bones.

Then came another problem. Big Henry had a unique and unacceptable notion. He wasn't given to rebellion. To the contrary, he embodied the proposition that a man will tolerate almost anything if he is bred and born to it. But Big Henry had a primitive desire to be a father to his child. There was no example for him to follow; no logical reason for his aspiration, other than the fact that Bones had been born of the woman he loved and was his own flesh and blood.

The concept of Big Henry as a father struck Gabriel Crow as heretical. Slavery made no provision for the recognition of parents. The master, not the father or mother, was the head of the family. The master, not the father or mother, set the rules and exercised authority when it came to raising children. Slaves were chattel with obligations to their master, not to family members. To the extent that slave parents spent time with their children, it was the mother who prepared meals and nurtured them. The father's primary parental function was breeding, nothing more.

Still, there is such a thing as a slave who will remain unbowed until he dies; whose bones can be broken, but whose spirit cannot be touched. Slavery as a system could make and change any law but the laws of nature. Big Henry refused to yield. And finally, Crow allowed him what was forbidden for other slaves—to be a father.

From the time Bones was old enough to walk, Big

Henry took him to the fields. Bones was permitted out of his father's sight only when he was with his mother. Big Henry loved him and nurtured him. And although Lilah became pregnant twice more, she never gave birth again.

Now though, there was another problem. Gabriel Crow was going mad. He was suffering from a form of dementia that robbed him of his ability to reason, yet reinforced all the prejudices and beliefs that fortified his exalted position of power.

In the antebellum South, public opinion and law acted as restraining influences on the cruelty of slave-owners. It was against the law for a master to deliberately kill a slave or cause a slave's death by excessive punishment. Life in prison could be imposed for such conduct, although lesser punishment was more common. In the case of a master who was brought to trial for shoving a knife into an insolent slave's eye, the master was found guilty of abuse and fined one hundred dollars. One doubts the court would have been so lenient had the situation been the other way around.

The power to punish was considered essential to slavery. Without a slave's fear of his master's retribution, obedience and discipline would cease to exist.

Whipping was the most common form of censure. Virtually all slaveholders employed the whip. Other punishments included imprisonment in a hole, diminished food rations, sale of the offending slave, and more creative penalties such as forcing a slave to eat the worms that he failed to pick off of crops. The state rarely intervened. Punishment was a private matter between a slave and his master.

Crow's dementia worsened as he aged, and he grew even more erratic. The same man who patted children on the head and gave them candy might order them sold the next day. The whipping of innocents grew more common, despite the accepted wisdom that scarred slaves dropped in value because potential buyers assumed them to be "trouble."

Then the dementia became paranoia. Crow grew obsessed with the fear of rebellion. "Slaves are horses," he wrote in his diary. "Horses with clothes and a religion. A horse with the strength of a dozen men will allow one man to beat him. But if there is one crevice through which a drop of doubt can fall regarding the absolute rightfulness of the relationship between master and slave, it will rust off the slave's chains."

Incidents of rebellion in the South were rare. In

1800, the year Big Henry was born, a Virginia slave named Gabriel Prosser had sought to create a slave army for an assault on Richmond. But before Prosser and his men could attack, a heavy storm flooded roads and washed out bridges. Two house servants betrayed the plotters before they could regroup and implement their plan. The conspirators were executed.

Two decades later, a former slave named Denmark Vesey spent four years stockpiling weapons and ammunition in anticipation of a slave revolt in Charleston, South Carolina. Like Prosser, Vesey was betrayed by house servants. One hundred and thirty-one slaves were arrested, and their leaders put to death.

Then, at the peak of Crow's paranoia, came the most frightening rebellion of all. In 1831, a Virginia slave named Nat Turner led seventy of his brethren from plantation to plantation, and murdered fifty-five members of slaveholding families. Federal and state troops crushed the rebellion. But in Crow's eyes, the damage had been done. He was now certain that his slaves meant to destroy him. To protect himelf, he commissioned a force of lower-caste white men, who roamed his plantation heavily armed. The most trivial offenses against order were met with brutal retribution.

Toenails were pulled from the feet of slaves who were disrespectful or moved too slowly. Fire was a slave's most potent weapon. Through arson, a slave could destroy his master's house and devastate a plantation. Thus, Crow decreed that fire would no longer be allowed for cooking in the slaves' quarters. Each slave was told that, should the master or a member of the master's family be assaulted, every slave on the plantation would die.

There was no protection against Gabriel Crow. Then he stepped over another boundary. Under the ungentle laws and customs of the South, it was the right of a man to make love to any slave girl he chose, so long as the slave's master consented. Generally, these sexual encounters fell between rape and fully consensual relations. Some slave women submitted to the advances out of fear or in the hope of special privileges. The rape of a slave girl was not a crime; only an offense against the master's property.

For his entire life, Gabriel Crow had refrained from sexual relations with his slaves. He lusted like other men, but his Christian beliefs forbade such encounters. Now, however, his resolve was weak. And in his madness, he could justify any desire.

On the eleventh of October 1831, Crow ordered that Lilah be brought to him. She fought. She struck blows. She refused to submit. As the struggle raged, the intensity of Crow's fury grew. Four of his men held Lilah down and spread her legs so he could enter. Her whole body lay exposed before him.

But then Crow's manhood failed him.

Gabriel Crow stood humiliated by a nigger woman. He would exact retribution.

The same men who had held Lilah down continued to hold her. Only now Crow's instrument of harm was a whip fashioned from untanned oxhide. The grip was an inch thick. From there, the weapon tapered over a three-foot length to a fine point that focussed the strength of arm and leather. One blow to any part of the body was enough to start blood flowing. Without a sound, Crow brought the lash down .... Again .... And again .... Flaying like a madman, mutilating every part of Lilah's body. One of the men who was holding her turned his face away in horror. But the mutilation continued, systematic and deadly, until both body and face were wounded beyond recognition. Then, barely breathing, Lilah was carried to the straw bed that she shared with Big Henry.

Big Henry, when told of the evil, tore wildly to his quarters and flung himself upon Lilah. There was a faint flickering of life in her body, but nothing more. He hung over her with moans and pleadings, kissed her, and implored her to speak, Her lips moved, but no sound came. Then she was still. She suffered no more.

Big Henry clenched his fists and raised them above his head in passionate emotion. "We was boy and girl together," he cried. "We was man and wife; she was mother to my son." Then his face grew hard. And without a sound, he raised himself up and began to run toward the great white house that Gabriel Crow lived in.

Crow had known that Big Henry would be coming. A dozen men stood on guard outside his home. Henry broke through them. The men regrouped, and rushed to join more of their number who were inside to repel his charge. After a struggle of Herculean proportions, Big Henry was subdued and chained. Only then did Gabriel Crow come out from hiding to face him.

Both men smelled of death. Big Henry strained to free himself from his bonds. Crow understood that one or the other of them must die.

Outside, in the fields, a large stake was driven into

the ground and a pile of scrap wood was assembled. Big Henry was stripped naked and roped to the stake. His muscles bulged and his skin seemed to glow. "You will burn in hell for eternity," Crow told him. "This is a taste of what you will endure."

Then Bones was brought to stand before them. The eyes of father and son met. The 31-year-old man and the eight-year-old boy.

The fanatical rage that had laid waste to Crow's mind was about to reach its ultimate horror.

The kindling was lit. The first smoke rose past Big Henry's face. There was terror in his eyes, but he refused to cry out. The wood was dry and burned rapidly. Flashes of flame sprang upward. Gabriel Crow laughed. The flames increased, growing ever higher. Bones watched as his father was enshrouded in smoke, until one final tide of flames burst forth and mercifully engulfed him.

Then Crow held a fire to Bones's face. But the child was innocent, and Crow was a good Christian. It would be wrong to kill him. Rather, he would sell Bones to another master and be done with Big Henry's brood forever. But one final precaution was essential. Big Henry's seed must be destroyed.

➤ ➤ ➤ ➤ ➤

Bones and I faced each other on the banks of the creek as he concluded his story. Grasping for words, he struggled to confirm the horror of what I now knew.

"They took off my clothes," Bones told me. "Crow brung the fire closer .... And he burned off the part that makes me a man."

CHAPTER 6

Bones's story lingered in my consciousness throughout our days together. Indeed, it has remained with me
through my entire life. But I was foolish and selfish
back then in the way that most young people are. And
the day Bones told it to me, something else was on my
mind. I was thinking about Nell Trimble.

At the community social the previous afternoon,
Nell had asked me to visit her sometime. The question
was when. I didn't want to make my attentions too
obvious. That would have been unsophisticated. But I
didn't want Nell to feel unattended to either. And I
was burning with desire to see her.

Finally, I worked out a little schedule in my mind.
The Fourth of July had fallen on a Wednesday. Friday
afternoon would be an appropriate time to visit; if I
could hold out that long.

Thursday passed very slowly. Thursday night, I had
trouble falling asleep. Accordingly, I slept later than

usual on Friday, which earned me a lecture from Pete about how the early bird catches the worm.

"Pete; that's an interesting proposition," I countered. "But the truth is, I have no use for worms. Besides, if a person really wants a worm, he can stay up late and catch one right before he goes to bed."

Pete had no rebuttal to that. Soon after, he and Widow Peaks went into town to pick up a few items at the general store. Meanwhile, Bones and I began the chores we were obligated to perform in exchange for food and lodging. We finished at noon. Then I lay down in the sun, intent upon watching the grass grow—

"Sam! Sam!"

Pete's shouting shattered the tranquility of the moment.

"Sam! I was in town, and I saw Nell."

"That's interesting," I said, trying to appear casual.

"She was at the general store." Pete's face was flushed with excitement, and he had the aura of one charged with an important mission. "Nell said 'Hello, Pete; how are you?' Then she wrote out a letter, and asked me to give it to you."

I waited.

Pete fumbled through his pants pocket for what

seemed an eternity, but probably wasn't more than three or four hours. Finally, he extracted a piece of paper that was crumpled up, not folded.

"Here it is. Nell said it was important, and made me promise to give it to you."

With excitement that I still remember, I uncrumpled the letter. It was written in an ornate but pleasing hand:

> Dear Mr. Clemens,
>
> It certainly was nice to make your acquaintance at the Independence Day gathering. If you don't think it too forward of me, I would like to invite you for dinner. Saturday evening at six would be nice. I hope you won't disappoint me.
>
> Sincerely,
> Nell Trimble

Life can be beautiful.

That night, I washed the best of my three shirts and hung it out to dry. Then, in the morning, I inspected the shirt and found it less than satisfactory. There was a tobacco stain that hadn't come out and a tear on the back of the collar.

Since I was anxious to make a good impression on Nell, I walked into town to the general store. The ready-made shirts were expensive, but I didn't have time to make my own. Besides, if the truth be known, I had no idea how to make a shirt, so I bought one. Then I stopped by The Silver Slipper to say hello to Miss Lurleen. Bones's performance on the Fourth of July had caused something of a stir, so I was greeted as a celebrity by the patrons at the bar. I had a drink and talked with a few of the townfolk. At precisely six o'clock that evening, I presented myself at Nell Trimble's door.

Nell's house stood in a lonely spot about two miles from town. From the outside, it appeared to have one large room, possibly with a storage loft. Nell answered the door when I knocked, and looked as beautiful as before. She was remarkably comely; trim yet rounded.

"Come in," she beckoned.

I entered and looked around. The room had a simple grace. Everything was spotless. The walls had pictures taken from books, mounted and positioned with care. Dolls and delicate feminine things adorned every available surface. There was a dressing table with a mirror set in a carved-wood frame. In the corner, next to the washstand, I saw a real china pitcher and bowl. It was the home of one who did what was possible within limited means to indulge tastes above the common.

The dinner table was comparably set. Nell's cooking was on the same high level as her decorative skills. At first, we talked about my favorite subject, which was Samuel Langhorne Clemens. But gradually, I began to probe about how it was that such a beautiful young woman was living alone on the prairie.

"It's nice of you to ask about me," Nell said, looking into my eyes. "I don't talk about my life often, but I'll tell you what you want to know."

There followed a story of suffering that touched me at my core. Nell's mother had been struck by a fever when Nell was five years old. It was the kind of fever that resembles fire; that bakes a woman's brain and burns the physical forces out of her. The fever took her life, and also the life of Nell's infant brother. After that, Nell and her father lived alone. When Nell was twelve, a drifter killed her father. "He was a crazy man; that's all he was. He stopped my father on the road, and shot him just to shoot him." Nell had lived since then on the meager savings left to her by her father. She was now in danger of losing her farm, because a thousand-dollar mortgage payment was due. She was eighteen years old; two years younger than I was.

After dinner, I settled in a comfortable chair. Nell sat at my feet, and we talked about whatever came to mind. I waxed eloquent on a play I'd read that was called Hamlet and had been written by William Shakespeare. I also touched on what little I knew about art and music.

Then Nell pointed to a tall cottonwood tree just outside the window. "Do you see that tree?"

"Yes."

"When I was a child, my father called that 'the happy tree.' Each year on my birthday, he tied ribbons around its branches and we had a party beneath it." Smiling at the memory, she went on, and I had the sense that she was leading up to something special. "I drew a picture of the tree once. I tried to put down on paper what I remembered about an ice storm that happened when I was young. Would you like to see it?"

"Yes."

Nell crossed the room and took what appeared to be

a diary from her dressing table. Then she returned to my side and opened the book to a page near the middle. "The Ice Storm" was written across the top of the page, above a pen-and-ink drawing of the tree with its naked limbs encased in hard pure ice so that the tree looked like a skeleton made of glass. A sheaf of rays from the sun was firing into the tree, giving the tiny icicles that hung from each twig and branch the appearance of glittering diamonds.

"Do you like it?" Nell asked.

"It's beautiful."

"Is that true; or are you just being polite?"

It was the truth, and I told her so.

"Sam; you make me feel so good."

And then Nell did something remarkable. She took the page between her forefinger and thumb, stared at the drawing as though giving one last thought to what she was about to do, and tore the page from her diary.

"I'd like you to have this. Carry it always, and think of me."

And in that moment, I was more in love than I had ever been before.

Nell fixed her emerald-green eyes upon me.

"Sam, I'd like you to kiss me."

I put my arm around her waist, and drew her close to me. Her face turned upward toward mine with a happy welcoming smile. I bent down, and she received my kiss as though it were natural to take pleasure in my offer. Then she removed the ribbon from her hair, and her auburn tresses fell free.

"Now you can kiss me better," she said.

I kissed her again, and again she spoke.

"You know the feeling that trembles through you when you see someone so enchanting and wonderful that it's a joy to be alive. And you know how a person gazes sometimes; how your throat goes dry and your breath comes up short, but you wouldn't want to be anywhere else on earth than where you are. Sam; I'm going to enjoy getting to know you."

The affection I felt for her was finer than any I'd known. I was twenty years old; at the pinnacle of my young life. And Nell Trimble had entered my heart. But as impossible as it seemed, the night was about to grow even more magical between us.

Nell took me by the hand and led me to her bed. "We can cuddle if you'd like," she said.

The bed had a blue-and-white spread on top and two pillows with white muslin cases. Nell lit a candle, and the flickering flame danced with a sheet of moon-light. She kissed me all over my face, and pressed her body against mine. I'd never known a happier time. My joy was near perfect.

Then Nell began to remove my clothes. And I had visions of staying with her forever. This would be my home till the end; or if I chose to wander, she would always be with me. The disrobing continued, mine and hers, until we lay naked together.

Nell gave me a peculiar smile. "This is the way we are," she said. Then she reached out, took hold of me, and guided me inside her body to a place where I'd never been before. I was just a boy. But she was girl and woman.

Moonlight streamed through the window. And in that moment, her face, which had been only humanly beautiful before, became divine.

Our bodies rocked back and forth. I could feel my excitement rising.

Then, suddenly, Nell blurted out, "Oh, no! Sam, we mustn't." Almost simultaneously, as she thrust herself forward, she pulled her lower body away from mine, so we were no longer joined together. And though the central act of our journey was incomplete, I knew I'd just traveled somewhere that would remain in my thoughts forever.

Impulsively, Nell rose from the bed. I watched, and she began to move; lithe and nubile; turning, swirling on her toes, like a prima ballerina.

She danced and danced, on and on. More than fifty years have passed since then. But I remember every turn and swirl as though I saw them yesterday. She danced and danced, it seemed, forever. Until finally, she dropped exhausted into my waiting arms.

That night, I slept with Nell on a bed of black velvet clouds and stars.

CHAPTER 7

The morning after my night with Nell, I was in for a rude awakening. Not the actual waking-up part. That was fine. But once we were awake, Nell announced that we were going to church together.

When I was a boy, my mother took me to church every Sunday. That was when I'd formed the view that, the less there is to justify a custom, the harder it is to get rid of it. Morals are an acquirement, and I know that some people find it hard to be good without a fear of God. But for those of us who are comfortable with our sins, attending church is an inestimable bother.

When we reached the church, I could see that just about everybody from town was there. Marshall Bassett was sitting with Miss Lurleen and Judith. Doc Fuller and his wife were talking with Ezra Moore. Pete and Widow Peaks were sitting a row behind Cowhand Bob. And so on down the line. Folks were wearing their Sunday best, and I was proud to be with Nell.

Pete looked over when we came in, and I thought I saw a touch of envy in his eyes. For a moment, he seemed to contemplate what he should and shouldn't do. Then he got up from his pew, and walked over to us with a flower in his hand.

"Hi, Nell. Hi, Sam."

Nell handled the moment with the diplomacy of one who was used to Pete's attentions.

"Pete; what a beautiful flower!" She took it, and with Pete still there, explained, "Every Sunday, Pete gives me the most beautiful flower. It's something I look forward to all week long."

"Nell; put the flower in your hair."

"Now, Pete; you always say that to me. And you know I hold your pretty flowers in my hand."

That seemed to satisfy Pete, who returned to his mother's side. Nell and I took seats in the back row, and the sermonizing began.

Actually, the preacher wasn't bad. My own childhood was filled with tales of delinquent boys who skipped church to go fishing on Sunday, drowned in a river, and were consigned to the fires of hell before the chill of the river was out of them. This sermon was more gentle. Nonetheless, I'll admit that my mind took to wandering. There was just too much talking and praying. We prayed for ourselves; we prayed for each other; we prayed for a dozen-or-so folks I'd read about in the Bible. And it occurred to me that the fellow we really ought to be praying for was Satan. After all, here was a man who for untold centuries had maintained a hold on most of the human race. Obviously, he had great executive ability, since he'd accomplished his works without a single salaried helper while the righteous opposition employed millions. He was a sinner who needed our prayers, but nobody prayed for Satan.

At the end of the sermon, the preacher passed a collection plate around the congregation. My first inclination was to let the plate pass without intervening in what I considered to be a local matter. But an uneasy conscience is like a hair in the mouth. And besides, I wanted to make a good impression on Nell, so I tossed a few coins on the platter. Then church was done and I took Nell home, looking forward to spending the afternoon with her.

The rest of the day, I performed various chores in and around Nell's home. I've often said that work is what we're obliged to do, whereas pleasure is what we do by choice. There are wealthy European noblemen who climb mountains at great cost to themselves and consider it play. But if offered wages for the same privilege, they'd consider it work and quit. Employing the standard just enunciated, my afternoon was spent at play. I fixed a window and chopped some wood and enjoyed every minute of it.

That night, I returned to Widow Peaks's farm; but only after acceding to Nell's request that I ride into town with her the next day. She needed some things from the general store, and said that my company would be desirable. The following afternoon, as agreed, Nell appeared at the widow's door. Pete was delighted to see her, and asked if he could join us. Nell said yes; I asked Bones if he wanted to come for the ride; and the four of us rode into town in the widow's horse and wagon.

Pete was in a fidgety state; as though weighing his jealousy with regard to Nell and myself against the fact that the same circumstances were now responsible for his spending extra time with her.

"Hey, Nell," he said as we made our way into town. "Remember, you promised you'd make me jam this summer."

"I know," Nell reassured him.

"I like strawberry jam. And I like peach jam and raspberry jam ...."

By the time Pete finished his litany of culinary tastes, we'd arrived in town and hitched the wagon in front of the general store.

"I'll be a while," Nell told me. "Why don't you go over to the saloon. I'll come and get you when I'm ready to go."

I said I'd be happy to stay with her, but she was pretty insistent. Meanwhile, Pete opted for going to the general store with Nell, and Bones chose to wait in the wagon. That left me on my own, so I went over to The Silver Slipper to say hello to whomever might be around. Mona and Judith were polishing the bannister that led to the second floor. Several of the locals were playing cards. Most of the faces at the bar were familiar.

I ordered a whiskey; and after a while, a fellow I hadn't seen before moved into the space beside me. He was tall and handsome in a hard sort of way, and looked about forty years old. His clothes were comfortable, but clean and well-made. He had the bearing of a prosperous rancher, which it turned out, was what he was.

His name was Lamar Hughes, and he was passing through town on the way home to his ranch forty miles to the south. We talked a bit about his business and what I was doing in Kansas. Then one of the townfolk joined us. That turned the conversation to the Fourth of July and my role in Bones's fistic triumphs. Hughes seemed uninterested at first, but after a while he got drawn into the talk. The local was expounding about Bones, and how he was different from other fighters. Finally, Hughes had had enough.

"You know, I've got a boy who works on my ranch. He's pretty tough; gets into fights in saloons on occasion. Wins some, loses some; but he can fight."

I nodded in understanding, knowing full well that there was a difference between the fighting Hughes was talking about and Bones's level of skill. But Hughes kept pressing. The liquor was getting to him. And finally, he uttered magic words: "I'd put some money on my fighter."

That piqued my interest, so I explained to Hughes how I set up matches. If Bones were to fight against his fighter, eighty percent of the proceeds from admission charges would go to the winner. The other twenty percent would be mine for orchestrating the fight.

That didn't seem completely fair to Hughes.

"Why should you get twenty percent?"

"I just told you; I'm the one who sets up the fight."

"Suppose I helped you arrange everything? Wouldn't ten percent for each of us be a fairer division of profit?" Before I could answer, Hughes went on like a barrister making his point. "You know, I'm not unfamiliar with business. I own a ranch. I deal with people all the time. I could help you draw a pretty big crowd, if your man and my man fought."

That was when Nell came into the saloon and announced she was ready to go home. Lamar Hughes looked at her approvingly, then back in my direction.

"I'll tell you what, Mr. Clemens. Let's make this interesting. Eighty percent of all the admission proceeds will go to the winning fighter, and the other twenty percent will go to the man who backs him."

Then Hughes added one more thought.

"Billy Morris is the name of my fighter. I'll wager a thousand dollars on him."

A thousand dollars! My fantasies were soaring. But then reality intervened.

"That's very nice, Mr. Hughes. But unfortunately, I don't have a thousand dollars."

"Sam; wait a minute!" The voice was Nell's. "Sam; I want to talk to you."

Nell gestured toward a corner of the saloon, where no one else was standing. I excused myself from Hughes, and walked with her to the spot she'd chosen where we could talk in private.

"Sam; what's he talking about; a thousand dollars?"

"It's a wager he wants to make."

"What kind of wager?"

"A fight between Bones and someone who works on his ranch. But it's only talk; I don't have a thousand dollars."

Nell's eyes were wide with passion approximating that of our rapturous night.

"Sam; I have a thousand dollars. That's the value of the deed on my ranch, separate and apart from the mortgage. And I need a thousand dollars more, or the bank will foreclose on the property."

"Nell; you don't understand. A thousand dollars is—"

She cut me off with a look that said I was the one who didn't understand.

"Sam; please! I know how Bones fights."

Lamar Hughes came over to join us.

"Mr. Hughes; I can't give you an answer yet. I need

some time to think this out."

"That's well and good," Hughes told me. "But I have to leave for home."

"Just give me a minute."

I ran outside, across the street to the wagon where Bones was waiting.

"Bones; I've got a question for you. There's a man in the saloon who has someone for you to fight. I want you to come with me, and tell me what you think about it."

With no idea of the stakes involved, Bones accompanied me back inside The Silver Slipper.

Hughes was talking with the bartender, and looked up as we entered. "Well, Mr. Clemens; what will it be?"

"Bones," I explained; "this man is named Lamar Hughes, and there's someone he wants you to fight. Most of the purse would go to the winner. But on top of that, Mr. Hughes wants to bet a thousand dollars against the deed to Nell's ranch on the outcome."

For a moment, Bones stood silent; the numbers spinning in his head. In all likelihood, he'd never held a twenty-dollar gold piece in his hand. The references he'd heard before to thousands of dollars were merely fanciful forms of speech. And now—

"That's a lot of money to be riskin'," Bones said. "I

reckon it depends on what the other feller's like."

But now Nell was possessed by a fervor born of desperation and hope. "Sam; I believe in Bones."

"I know," I said. "But the risk—"

"I'll ask Pete."

"You'll what?" I said incredulously.

"I'll ask Pete. He spent some time south of here last year, when Widow Peaks was sick. They had a doctor there; a good doctor, better than Doc Fuller."

Before I had a chance to respond, Nell was out the door.

Lamar Hughes looked at me, shook his head, and smiled. "That's a pretty woman you've got there, son."

Moments later, Nell was back with Pete at her side.

"Pete; I want to ask you something," she said. "Last year, when your mother was sick, you took her about fifty miles south. When you were there, did you know a cowhand named . . . . Damn, what's his name?"

"Billy Morris," Lamar Hughes offered.

"That's right. Did you know a cowhand named Billy Morris?"

I expected Pete to furrow his brow, but instead, his visage darkened. "Billy Morris. I don't like Billy Morris."

"Why not?"

"Billy Morris was always pickin' on me. Then one of the cowhands beat him up."

"Who beat him up?" Nell pressed.

"One of the cowhands. Billy Morris is real mean, and he drinks a lot. He bullied me until folks there said he ought to stop. Then he got in a fight, and the other fellow punched him in the stomach, and Billy fell down and started chokin' for air. And I saw him in another fight, where he got hit in the mouth and quit."

"Mr. Hughes," I said. "It sounds to me as though your fighter's not as tough as you think."

"That's a matter of opinion, Mr. Clemens."

"Please, Sam; make the deal," Nell pressed.

"All right. Mr. Hughes; you've got yourself a wager."

"Fine. Let's put it in writing."

Quite a few onlookers had gathered, so we moved to a table in the corner. I sat in the same chair I'd occupied two weeks earlier when I'd won Bones playing poker. A good omen.

In negotiating, a man almost always refuses another man's first offer. But here, most of the things to be negotiated were pretty straightforward. We agreed that the fight would be held five days hence, on Saturday,

July fourteenth. The winner would receive all of the admission money. There was a side wager of one thousand dollars, and the London Prize Ring Rules would be followed.

Midway through the negotiations, Miss Lurleen came downstairs and asked what was going on. I told her, and she shook her head.

"Sam; folks around here mind their own business. But are you sure you know what you're doing?"

"This man's not running a saloon," Hughes told her. "This young man is a player."

Next, we determined a site for the fight. "How about Hood Canyon?" Hughes offered.

I didn't know where Hood Canyon was. But the bartender said it was about ten miles from town and as good a place as any to fight.

Then Bones was heard from. "I don't want no throwin'," he told me. "No throwin', no wrestlin'; none of that."

"Put it in the contract," I said.

For the first time, Hughes's eyes showed resistance. "I guess your man is afraid of a real fight." I didn't answer, so he piled on more bait. "Are you letting a colored dictate what you negotiate?"

"I reckon so, since he's the one who'll be fighting."

"And don't forget the referee," Miss Lurleen cautioned. "You want someone who will call a fair fight."

I looked at Bones.

"The marshall," he said.

One of the townfolk went over to the jail, and reported back that Marshall Bassett would referee the fight.

"And not to insult you," I told Hughes. "But how do I know you'll pay the thousand dollars after Bones wins on Saturday?"

"The same way I know I'll collect my money after Billy Morris knocks your man out. By Wednesday at noon, my thousand dollars and your pretty woman's deed will be put in escrow at the bank."

In less than an hour, the contract was negotiated, and Hughes wrote out two copies on separate sheets of paper:

Articles of Agreement entered into this 9th day of July 1856 between Lamar Hughes and Sam Clemens

The signatories to this contract agree to a stand-up fight between Billy Morris, white and twenty-one years of age, and Bones, colored and approximately thirty-three years of age, on the following terms and conditions:

1. The fight will be held at Hood Canyon at 10:00 o'clock on the morning of Saturday, July fourteenth.

2. The winner of the fight will be entitled to all money from the sale of admission to the fight.

3. Should Bones win the fight, Lamar Hughes will pay to Sam Clemens the additional sum of one thousand dollars. This amount will be placed in escrow within two days of the signing of this contract.

4. Should Billy Morris win the fight, Sam Clemens will pay to Lamar Hughes the additional sum of one thousand dollars. This amount will be collateralized in the first instance by the deed to property owned by Miss Nell Trimble.

5. The fight shall take place on turf in an enclosure twenty feet squared formed by eight stakes and ropes. The ropes shall

extend in double lines, the uppermost rope being four feet from the ground and the lower rope being two feet from the ground.

6. A mark shall be drawn in the center of the enclosure as the scratch. Spaces sufficiently large to hold a fighter and two seconds between rounds shall be enclosed by other marks in the turf in opposite corners.

7. The fight shall consist of an undetermined number of rounds. A round shall end when a combatant is down. Once down, a combatant has thirty seconds to come to scratch or lose the fight. Falling without receiving a legitimate blow shall be grounds for disqualification at the referee's discretion. Striking a fallen combatant when he is down shall also be grounds for disqualification at the referee's discretion.

8. No butting, gouging, biting, hitting below the waist, or throwing shall be allowed.

9. The decision of the referee shall be final with regard to all matters not otherwise specified in this contract. The referee

for the fight shall be Marshall John Bassett.

Nell signed both copies of the contract in the margin beside clause number four. Lamar Hughes and I signed at the bottom.

We shook hands.

"All right, Mr. Clemens," Hughes told me. "I'll see you on Saturday morning at ten o'clock."

🐦 🐦 🐦 🐦 🐦

After my business with Lamar Hughes was done, I got in the wagon with Nell, Bones, and Pete. Nell was anxious to get home, and seemed on edge about the day's events. That was understandable, since the fate of her farm was wholly dependent upon Bones's fists.

Meanwhile, Pete was his usual self. And due to the uncertainty of the moment, he was sorely trying Nell's patience.

"Nell! Nell! Did I do all right when Sam asked me about Billy Morris?"

"You were very helpful," Nell assured him.

"Was I a big help?"

"Pete; I don't want to talk about it," she snapped. But then her voice softened and she added, "Now,

Pete, when I make jam for you next week, what kind of jam would you like?"

When we reached Nell's farm, I walked her to the door and kissed her gently on the lips. She held my hand, then let it drop. "Bones will win, won't he?" she asked.

"Don't worry. Bones knows how to fight, and Billy Morris doesn't."

That satisfied her for the moment. We said goodbye, and I rode back to Widow Peaks's farm with Bones and Pete. When we got there, Pete ran into the house, and I went to the barn with Bones to discuss the upcoming fight. There wasn't much for him to do in preparation for the bout. Sleep well; eat right; spend some extra time each day stretching his muscles and limbering up. The important thing would be to not let Billy Morris get lucky early. Once Bones repulsed his early charges and Morris realized the difference between barroom brawling and a real fight, the end would be near.

Around six o'clock, Widow Peaks called us for dinner. I wasn't particularly hungry, and I still hadn't gotten used to the widow's cooking. Also, Nell was on my mind; so rather than eat, I decided I'd walk back to her place and tell her again not to worry.

It was the time of year with long days and short nights, and the early evening sky was light. Wild roses and columbine were in bloom. A jackrabbit scurried by. I picked a few berries along the way, and washed them down with water from the creek.

When I reached Nell's house, I knocked on the door.

There was no response, so I knocked again.

"Nell! Are you home?"

There was still no answer.

Maybe she was asleep.

I opened the door. And in that moment, the coldest sensation I've felt in my entire life passed through me. It was as though the sky had crumbled and collapsed with a crash, leaving the earth in ruins.

Nell was sitting at the same table we'd had dinner at two nights before.

Two men were sitting with her.

Lamar Hughes was to her right.

And to her left sat Hiram Kane.

Kane laughed; a loud booming laugh that soared to the heavens, but sounded as though it had been fashioned in Hades.

"Hello, Sam," he said.

My mind had trouble focussing. It was as though some kind of chemical substance had been released in my brain and was jumbling my thoughts.

Nell stared down at the table.

There was silence.

Finally, Lamar Hughes spoke.

"I'm a businessman, Sam. That's all," he said. "Two weeks ago, Mr. Kane came to me with a proposition. He said someone had cheated him in a card game. And he told me about a young man down in Mississippi named Billy Morris. All I had to do was put up the money to bring Billy here for a fight. That and a few other details, like you and me getting our contract signed. Nell, who's a friend of mine, helped close that part of the deal. I talked with her about the situation right around the Fourth of July, and she's been quite helpful."

I didn't understand what was happening. Hughes went on in response to the look of confusion in my eyes.

"Nell and I are partners on this. It's quite simple, really. Bones and Billy Morris fight. Billy wins. Then Nell, Mr. Kane, and I split the profits."

"Don't be sure Billy wins," I said defiantly. "From

what Pete says, Billy's not—"

Then I realized, it wasn't just Nell.

Pete would do anything for me. That was what Nell had said when I met her at the Fourth of July social.

"Like I was saying," Hughes continued. "Nell, Mr. Kane, and I are partners. When the fight is over, the two of them will divvy up the admission money. As for me; there's the matter of our little side bet in the amount of one thousand dollars."

Something wasn't making sense. Nell had pledged the deed to her farm as collateral for the wager. Why would she—

"I know what you're thinking," Hughes said. His words were flowing now in a combination of explanation and bragging. "You're telling yourself, all that will happen is Nell will lose her farm. That's where this gets interesting. The deed that Nell pledged today is one hundred percent worthless. Her farm is worth, at most, eighteen hundred dollars. And right now, she owes the bank more than nineteen hundred on her mortgage. Read the contract you signed, Sam. It says, 'Should Billy Morris win the fight, Sam Clemens will pay to Lamar Hughes the additional sum of $1,000. This amount will be collateralized in the first instance by the deed to property owned by Miss Nell Trimble.' In the first instance, Sam. That means, if the deed's no good, you owe me the money."

"You're wasting your time, Mr. Hughes. I don't have a thousand dollars."

Hughes smiled. "I know that, Sam. But you have something just as good as money. You own a nigger named Bones. You see, from what I understand, you never formally signed any freedom papers. And under the law, if a man doesn't get the formalities of a situation right, the moralities of it don't matter. So in five days, I'm going to own me a fine fighting nigger. I know he'll fetch a handsome price down in Mississippi or Alabama."

"The fight's not over. Bones could win."

For the first time, Kane interrupted. "Sam, let me tell you about your nigger. Bones is old. Thirty-three years is old for fighting. He's got some skills, but he's tired and worn down. Billy Morris is young. He outweighs your nigger by more than forty pounds. And I'll tell you some more about Billy. There's a man in Mississippi named Robert Clennell, who owns a plantation and hundreds of slaves. Clennell pays the slaves to fight Billy. That is, he pays the winner. If the nigger wins, he gets five hundred dollars. Do you know what five hundred dollars means to a slave? Five hundred dollars is halfway to a nigger buying his freedom. Five hundred dollars is the start of a new life. And poor Billy; when Billy wins, all he gets is one hundred dollars. And you know something, Sam? Billy has never lost a fight. Some of the niggers Billy has fought have been trained to fight pretty good; just like your nigger. But Billy beats those fancy niggers. Billy Morris has been trained to fight. Billy Morris knows how to hurt people. At first, they matched him against weak niggers. Then he got good at hurting, so they started matching him against strong ones. Four months ago, Billy got matched against a nigger in Atlanta; strongest nigger they had in Georgia. Billy beat that nigger good; beat him some more; pushed the bone of his nose into his brain. That's the second man I know of that Billy Morris killed in a fight. But the first one don't count, because the first one was one of those weak niggers."

Now Lamar Hughes was talking. "You can't run, Sam. Don't even think about it. If you run, you forfeit and handbills will go up all over the territory: 'Reward, One Hundred Dollars. Runaway slave, thirty-three years old. Five-feet-eight-inches tall, one hundred forty pounds. Answers to the name of Bones. Distinguishing physical characteristics; scar over left eye, missing three teeth. And oh, yes; an important part of his body is missing.'"

Kane laughed. "Sam; I told you before we started playing poker; you can lose a large amount of money when you gamble with me. You're a good card cheat, but I'm smarter than you are. Don't you ever hustle me."

Through it all, Nell had been silent. Now I turned to face her.

"How could you do this?"

"Sam; I'm sorry."

"I thought you loved me."

There was no response.

"How much of what you told me was true?"

"Some of it."

"Which parts?"

"It doesn't matter."

My throat was starting to choke up. I felt what a soldier must feel when a bullet crashes through his heart. I began to cry. Tears streamed down my cheeks.

And then Nell said something that to this day remains the cruelest thing that anyone has ever said to me: "Sam, why don't you go outside so you can have this private time to yourself."

There was nothing more for me to do in this truly godforsaken place. I began to leave, and at the door, turned for one last look.

Nell and Lamar Hughes were smiling at each other.

Hiram Kane was looking at me. The fires of Hell burned in his eyes.

I shall never be as miserable again as I was that night. My grief was desolating, and my pain was sharp. My young innocence had been shattered and could never be restored.

I'd believed in Nell's love because I had wanted to believe. I'd seen only her exterior beauty; not the person inside. She had fixed her emerald-green eyes upon me like a cat stalking its prey. I can see that now, because I am white-headed now. I understand that my feelings for her were not true love. Yet no woman has ever done more to furnish me with a broken heart.

It was a cold world I walked in that night. I had not known that temperature before. I walked alone for hours and hours. And finally, when sunrise came, the sky was gray and sad.

CHAPTER 8

Bones was awake and had begun to exercise outside the barn when I returned to Widow Peaks's farm. I intended to wait until he finished before telling him what had happened. But I must have looked ghastly sick, because as soon as he saw me, he stopped and asked what was wrong.

We sat together on a bale of hay, and I told him what a fool I'd been. I explained what kind of fighter Billy Morris was, and that there was no way we could run. Bones understood the gravity of the situation. But he didn't berate me. He just listened. Nothing that grieves us can be called small. By the laws of proportion, a child's loss of a doll and a king's loss of his crown are events of the same size. Bones was facing a loss of staggering proportions; the loss of his freedom. And I was amazed at the calm unaccusing nature of his reaction.

It was Tuesday morning, and the fight was scheduled for Saturday at ten o'clock. I wasn't sure how to proceed, but one thing was certain. I didn't want to be anywhere near Pete any more. That meant finding someplace else to stay. I could go back to The Silver Slipper, but Bones might not be welcome there. We could camp out by the creek, but that wouldn't be comfortable; and I wanted Bones to be as comfortable as possible. So we sat together, wondering what to do, while I told myself that an enemy can partly ruin a man but it takes an injudicious ally to make the job perfect.

Then I saw Cowhand Bob on his horse riding toward us.

"Howdy, Sam."

"Hello, Cowhand Bob. What brings you this way?"

"I was in town and saw Hiram Kane. He was laughing and bragging, talking about how some fellow from Mississippi was gonna put Bones in his place, and how Miss Nell had hoodwinked you. I didn't like the way things sounded, so I thought I'd come by and see if you needed help."

"Cowhand Bob; you're a very sweet fellow."

"Thank you, Sam. Folks around here pride themselves on being nice."

Our most immediate need was a place to stay. Cowhand Bob said he didn't think it would be a problem for us to spent the next four nights at his boss's ranch, so I went into the widow's house to pack my belongings. Pete was there, and pretended not to see me. He had the look of a dog that has soiled its master's home, knows it, and wants to avoid punishment. I packed in silence, not acknowledging his presence. Then, on the way out, I stopped just long enough to say, "Pete; you're a fat stupid ugly pig." He didn't answer.

An hour later, Bones and I were on the Lazy Bird Ranch. There we began the routine we would follow for the next four days. Bones hung a sack of wheat from the barn rafters and pounded on it to sharpen his punching. Then he marked off an area outside the barn, twenty feet squared. I stood with him, throwing punches, and he moved to escape them; dodging, blocking, bobbing, weaving. At times I was unsure why he moved in a particular way. But discretion being the better part of valour, I decided it was better to keep my mouth closed and appear stupid than to open it and remove all doubt.

One thing though, was abundantly clear. The first

rule of being a fighter is, nothing short of perfection will suffice. Every mistake leaves a fighter vulnerable to attack by an opponent who knows how to strike. Yet no fighter is perfect; all fighters get hit. Thus, in facing Billy Morris, Bones would need a calm cool courage that no peril or pain could shake.

The Lazy Bird Ranch was an attractive spread with a dozen cowhands, a stable-boy, and a cook. Mr. Harrison, who was the owner, welcomed us and then went about his business. We ate with the cowhands. And we slept in the barn, but that was because the bunkhouse was full; not because of Bones's color. In fact, two of the cowhands who lived in the bunkhouse were colored.

Wednesday, after Bones finished his practice, I rode into town. My main interest in going was the hope that Lamar Hughes had failed to put his thousand-dollar escrow payment in the bank. That would have voided our contract, but unfortunately the money was there.

So was Hiram Kane. He and Hughes had taken over the selling of the fight, and I'd never seen anything like it. They'd printed up handbills showing a woodcut of two fighters; one black, the other white. The circular promised "championship boxing" between

Billy Morris—referred to as "The Fighting Angel"—
and Bones. The time and place of the bout were listed,
as was the admission charge. One dollar! The equivalent of two days' wages.

Kane was standing outside the saloon, offering
handbills to everyone who passed. "This Saturday, at
Hood Canyon," he shouted. "Come see a fight to the
finish between The Fighting Angel, young Billy
Morris, against a man possessed by the Devil. There
will be excitement like the Kansas territory has never
seen before. The champion of the South, Billy Morris,
will dare to challenge the demon who has terrorized
the county."

Kane saw me as I crossed the street. "Well, lookee
here," he chortled. "It's the great white massuh; Sam
Clemens."

I should have kept walking. And after a moment's
pause, I did. But I'd hesitated just long enough to give
Kane encouragement. It was a rule of the South, and
also the border states, that a black person never looked
a white person directly in the eye. Kane adhered to that
rule with authority figures, but I was accorded no such
deference. He moved in front of me and blocked my
passage.

"Sam," Kane said, lowering his voice to make his remarks more private. "Listen to me, Sam. I'm talking to you straight. Your nigger is gonna get hurt."

"You never talked straight to anyone in your life. Take the lies out of you, and you'd shrink to the size of your hat."

"Lies? Sam; what lies? You might not like what I say, but when did I ever lie to you?"

Now I was hooked.

"I love you, Sam. I love all white people. I might have told a few lies in my life, because lying is the universal language of man. But Sam; I never lied to you."

His eyes were full of treachery and malice.

I shouldered my way past him and left.

Back at the ranch, I did some work around the barn as a way of earning my keep. Then I went to the creek to bathe. After that, Bones and I joined the cowhands for dinner. When the meal was over, I took a walk. Days begin early during the summer in Kansas, and most people go to bed at dark to be up at dawn the following morning. Still, I had some time to wander.

Cowhand Bob walked with me. "You can learn a lot about fighting by watching chickens," he said as we passed the chicken coop. "A good game rooster stays in front of its opponent and moves its head all the time. That keeps the other bird worrying about when the rooster will attack."

We came to the bunkhouse. A solitary voice accompanied by a guitar was singing:

> *She cheated on me all the time; she broke*
> *my heart in two*
> *She lied the day she told me that she*
> *always would be true*
> *Then she went and left me; so I sit at home*
> *and pine*
> *She's someone else's problem now, but I*
> *wish that she were mine.*

That brought my thoughts back to Nell, and Cowhand Bob responded to the look in my eyes.

"I know what happened with you and Nell Trimble," he said. "I don't mean to pry into your life. But when it comes to losing that woman, you shouldn't feel bad."

I didn't answer, but I didn't mind Cowhand Bob talking about the situation either. I guess he sensed that sentiment, because he kept talking.

"If you want my opinion, Nell is pretty but she's too skinny for comfort. And most folks stay away from her, because she uses people. This is a place where folks pride themselves on helping each other out. And Nell has a reputation for not being very nice."

I nodded in understanding, and Cowhand Bob went on.

"Now, if I could have me a wife, the woman I'd want is Miss Lurleen. A lot of us in the bunkhouse spend time thinking about her."

The sky was darkening as the sun set. Night insects were beginning to be heard.

"Mona will do you for a price. Judith, I'm not sure about. But I never heard of Miss Lurleen doing anyone." Cowhand Bob lowered his voice in dramatic fashion, indicating that my knowledge of life was about to be augmented. "One night, about a year ago, I was in town real late. The saloon was closed but I heard laughing inside, so I peeked in through the window. Miss Lurleen and Judith were sitting at the bar. They was drinking some kind of fancy wine. And they was naked."

"Naked?"

"That's what I saw. They was sitting and laughing and they reached out and touched hands. Then they got up and went upstairs on that big staircase going to the second floor."

Off in the distance, I saw Bones approaching.

Cowhand Bob saw him too.

"I don't know if it's right to talk about Miss Lurleen in front of a colored," he said. "Maybe we should change the conversation."

The next day was Thursday, two days before the fight. Bones went through his usual morning exercises. That afternoon, he undertook his most important practice session for the fight. The two previous days, I'd thrown punches in his direction to help sharpen his reflexes. But Billy Morris was a massive presence, and I was rather scrawny. Bones needed a sparring partner who was more imposing than I was. I'd mentioned the matter to Cowhand Bob, who concluded there was one person at a nearby ranch who was roughly Billy's size.

"But I'm not sure it would be right to ask him," Cowhand Bob told me.

"Why not?"

"It's Jason Trapp."

The name meant nothing to me until Cowhand Bob added, "Bones fought Jason on the Fourth of July, and beat him up pretty good."

Nonetheless, after due deliberation, Cowhand Bob

decided to ask Jason Trapp about sparring. And to my delight, Jason said he'd serve in a modified capacity. That is, he'd be happy to throw punches at Bones but not receive them.

Thursday afternoon, at Bones's instruction, I wrapped both of Jason's fists with long strips of cotton. Then he and Bones entered the square that had been marked off outside the barn. For about an hour, stopping occasionally to rest, Jason threw punches. Some of them landed; most missed. At the end of the session, I thanked him for his help, and Jason wished Bones good luck.

Friday was a day of rest. One of the cowhands who'd been away from the ranch reported back that handbills for the fight had been distributed throughout the county by one of Lamar Hughes's employees. We also learned that about fifty people from Mississippi had traveled north, intending to show their support for Billy Morris at the fight.

Late that afternoon, I spoke again with Cowhand Bob.

"Cowhand Bob; you've been good to me, but there's one more favor I'd like to ask."

Cowhand Bob indicated that he was listening.

"I've gotten into water that's way over my head. The fight's tomorrow. Both fighters will be allowed two seconds in the ring. And I was wondering if you'd be willing to serve as Bones's other second."

"Sam; I'd be truly honored."

"Thank you, Cowhand Bob. I appreciate it."

After dinner, most everyone on the ranch drifted back to the bunkhouse. Bones and I sat down together outside the barn. My nerves were on edge. I looked toward the sky. No ornament in the world compares in beauty to the moon and stars at night. They've dazzled man from the beginning of time, and will do so as long as we live.

As night approached, I turned toward Bones.

"Are you scared?"

"Yes."

The honesty of his response caught me by surprise. To believe oneself brave is to be brave. It is essential.

But courage is resistance to fear, mastery of fear; not absence of fear.

"What I hope," Bones said, "is I don't get hit hard too many times, or with two hard punches together. And I gotta find out about Billy Morris. Can he stand up to a punch? A lot of punches? If I hit him and hurt him, what comes next?" Bones laughed, a soft ironic laugh. "Ain't nothing wrong with takin' advantage of the other side in war. Fightin' is about hurtin' other people and survivin' when you get hurt."

Fireflies were flickering in the twilight. One of them flew past my head, testament to the proposition that nature never sleeps.

There was silence between us.

"Bones; I want to apologize for getting you into this mess."

"It don't matter. You done your best. All I want is to know the rules, what the situation is in front of me.

There was a purity to his thoughts; yet my own thoughts were jumbled. When an animal inflicts pain, it does so in innocence. It doesn't understand right from wrong, nor does it impart pain for the pleasure of causing it. But man does, knowing it to be pain. And alone among the earth's creatures, man enslaves and kills for sport. The fleets of the world could sail in comfort on the innocent blood our breed has spilt.

And I was part of it; the development of "civilization." It began in the Garden of Eden, with Abel praying at his altar. Cain approached his brother from behind. There was a crash of blows and shrieks and moans. Then silence. Abel lay in his own blood, the life gasping out of him. Cain stood over him, looking down; vengeful and unrepentant. Then came the Hebraic Wars. The Egyptian Wars. The Greek Wars. The Roman Wars. Christianity and Civilization marched hand in hand, leaving death and desolation in their wake. Other religions followed in kind. Each slaughter was more devastatingly effective than the one that had come before it. Cain had murdered with a club. The Hebrews killed with slings and swords. The Greeks and Romans added protective armor and the fine art of military generalship. Christians perfected guns. Against that backdrop of evolution, there was something primitive yet noble about two men stripped almost naked, each of them a willing participant, doing battle with their fists.

The stars came into view. They seemed much smaller than the earth, and the moon looked larger than any star. That's how the nighttime sky appeared to those who'd viewed it over the millenia.

"Heaven is somewhere up there," I said. "Bones; what will you do in Heaven?"

"I don't know. I guess I'll have me a farm ... if there be such a place as Heaven." The words were spoken with hesitation; as though I were being tested.

"I think there's a Heaven," I said. "Not hell. After bad people die, I believe they just cease to exist. But I think good people survive in some other dimension."

We talked until it was completely dark except for the moon and stars. Then we went into the barn to go to sleep, and I wished Bones a good night.

"Pleasant dreams," I said.

"Sam; I don't got dreams. I got nightmares."

And I realized how little I knew about this man; but what I knew about him, I liked. I'd become aware that Bones, despite his color, was a member of the human race.

That might not seem like much, but it was a very important discovery for me to make. Some people say that man is the noblest of God's creations. Of course, the folks who say that are members of the species. Personally, I prefer roses.

Still, I had come to understand that Bones was a very special person.

In a matter of hours, he would be fighting for his freedom. And I knew that, whatever happened the following day, I would carry it with me for the rest of my life.

CHAPTER 9

Bones and I both slept poorly on Friday night. My worries kept me awake long after I lay down my head. And judging by the sound of Bones's breathing, he was equally unsuccessful in sleeping.

We awoke at dawn. Bones was quieter than usual, and I left him to his thoughts. He ate a light breakfast and I did the same.

After breakfast, we returned to the barn and Bones emptied the sack that held his belongings. Some underclothing, an extra shirt; a knife, fork, spoon, and tin plate. All the possessions he owned on earth. At the bottom of the sack, he found what he wanted. Worn leather shoes, faded black breeches, and a pair of black stockings. His fighting outfit.

Bones put the fighting clothes on, and draped a shirt over his shoulders.

Cowhand Bob arrived at the barn shortly before eight o'clock. He'd gone into town and bought a jar of leeches from Doc Fuller. If Bones's eyes swelled up during the fight, the leeches could be applied to suck out the blood afterward. Once attached, they'd feed until bloated. Then they'd fall off; or if they refused to detach, they could be burned away.

At eight o'clock, Bones, Cowhand Bob, and I climbed onto one of The Lazy Bird's wagons. Cowhand Bob held the reins and I sat next to him. Bones got in back and, to conserve his energy, lay down beside four large buckets of water.

There was a procession of sorts to the fight site; a flow of wagons and riders on horseback from neighboring ranches and farms. Bones lay still with his eyes closed. At one point, I asked if he was asleep. He opened an eye and told me to leave him alone.

Shortly before ten o'clock, we arrived at Hood Canyon. It wasn't a canyon so much as a ravine; a desolate narrow river bed that had gone dry centuries before. Scarred walls ascended from a natural amphitheatre. The walls were dreary, save for one tiny flower growing straight out of a crack. A solitary forget-me-not without a droop about it, brandishing its bright blue star with the most gallant spirit in the world. I leaned forward to pick the flower. Surely, it was an omen. Then I realized, if I severed the flower from its root, it would die. It had survived this long, so I let it be.

At the bottom of the ravine, a boxing ring had been erected on a small patch of thin grass. Lamar Hughes had supervised its construction, and everything appeared to be in order. Four ropes extended at knee and chest height between stakes driven into the ground. Outside the ring, a second series of ropes cordoned off an area that would serve as a moat between the fighting and the crowd. In the center of the ring, a two-foot line had been carved into the dirt—the scratch.

Hughes's men had scoured the territory for spectators, and the fruits of their labor were clear. At least five hundred onlookers had gathered. Some of the faces were familar; most were not. Many came from the southern part of Kansas, where pro-slavery sentiment was strong. At least fifty had journeyed from Mississippi with Billy Morris. There were no women. All of the spectators were white.

The geography of Hood Canyon made it possible to bar entry to anyone who didn't pay. Two rough-looking cowhands from Hughes's ranch collected a dollar from each person approaching the site. There was a lot of wagering back and forth; mostly on which fighter would win and, to a lesser degree, on who would draw first blood. A sense of anticipation rippled through the air.

Hiram Kane stood just outside the ring. Our eyes met and he nodded.

Then I saw a huge well-muscled man with the face of a boy; a mean boy. He was wearing a black bowler hat, crimson breeches, and a crimson robe unbelted to reveal a thick neck and well-developed chest. His nose had been broken several times, which meant he had tasted pain and was willing to come back for more. He moved gracefully for one his size, with an aura of primeval strength, like a tiger. Bones saw him the moment I did. We both knew it was Billy Morris.

Marshall Bassett stepped into the ring, and paced off the distance between the stakes to satisfy himself that the fighting area was roughly twenty feet squared. At precisely ten o'clock, he signaled for the fighters to come forward. Billy Morris took off his bowler hat, tossed it over the top ring rope, and entered the enclosure. Lamar Hughes and a compatriot of Billy's from Mississippi followed. Bones was next, accompanied by

Cowhand Bob and myself. It was an electric moment. My heart was pounding.

The marshall tossed a coin to determine which fighter would get which corner. Hughes won and chose to position his team facing south. Billy's other second, the man from Mississippi, tied a crimson handkerchief to the post in Billy's corner.

The fighters stripped to their fighting clothes, and moved to within inches of each other. Billy was the larger of the two. His body was magnificently sculpted. Bones was visibly older.

Hazy sunlight beat down from above.

"I've heard about you," Billy said, looking hard into Bones's eyes.

Bones didn't answer.

"They say you're good."

He is, I started to say, but didn't. I held my tongue, because I knew instinctively that Bones didn't want my voice.

The marshall gave final instructions regarding the conduct of the fight: "Each round will end when a combatant is down. Once down, a man has thirty seconds to come to scratch or be declared the loser. No butting, gouging, hitting below the waist, or throwing is allowed. Are there any questions?"

There were none.

Bones's eyes looked different now from the way I'd seen them before. They were just as hard and just as cruel as those of Billy Morris. Both men seemed possessed and prepared for nothing less than war.

A tremor of excitement swept through the crowd as five hundred onlookers awaited the marshall's next word.

"Time!"

The fighters touched hands. Bones stepped back, and Billy Morris bore forward. Bones's left hand shot out. Each time I'd seen him fight before, he'd started with a jab. In addition to inflicting damage, it helped determine the speed and general ability of his opponent. Billy moved his head to the side, and the jab slid harmlessly by. A second jab landed. Billy jabbed back, shooting his left hand forward, squeezing his fist at the moment of impact for maximum effect. As soon as he scored, he pulled his hand back into a defensive posture; the same technique Bones had employed seconds earlier.

Suddenly, Billy Morris leapt forward, turning his left shoulder and body at the waist. His left arm traveled in an arc with lightning speed. Bones reacted, but a fraction of a second too late. The blow caught him high on the forehead, pushing him off balance. He stumbled backward and another glancing blow sent him tumbling to the ground.

The crowd roared.

Marshall Bassett stepped between the two men. Bones picked himself up without assistance, and the combatants returned to their corners. No physical damage had been done, but the impact on each fighter's mind was another matter.

In the corner, Cowhand Bob took a towel and wiped the back of Bones's neck. Bones looked across the ring, and said simply, "His hands are faster than I thought."

"Time!"

The combatants moved to scratch again, and resumed the early pattern of the fight. Billy was the aggressor, but it was controlled aggression; not a wild brawling assault. Bones kept moving, striking swiftly with his jab, followed by a defensive retreat. For the most part, both men aimed at soft targets. Blows to the head risked damage to the hands; and hands had to be preserved, since reality dictated the likelihood of a long fight. Still, when an opening presented itself, neither man was reluctant to punch forcefully to the head. Bones continued to jab in the direction of Billy's eyes.

Neither fighter showed emotion on his face. No fear, no hatred, no anger. I wondered if soldiers looked this way when they hardened and grew accustomed to battle. Bones seemed to be conserving energy; evading, moving, waiting for his opponent to tire. But Billy's constant aggression demanded that Bones expend energy too.

Billy missed with a leaping left hook, stumbled, and fell to the ground. Again, no damage had been done. But now, both fighters had felt the dirt.

Cowhand Bob wiped Bones's neck again, and I gave him a sip of water. Bones looked across the ring at Billy, as he'd done one round before. "I can hurt him," he said.

"Time!"

The fighters moved to the center of the ring. Bones picked up the tempo with his jab, keeping Billy off balance and creating openings for other blows. Billy was doing many of the things I'd seen Bones do before. Moving his head, blocking punches with his forearms and elbows. Faking blows to force Bones to reveal his defensive intentions. This was fighting at a higher level of skill than I had ever seen.

Bones landed his jab again. A trickle of blood appeared just above Billy's left eye.

"First blood!" Hiram Kane shouted. "The claret rushes forth."

Cheers and groans emanated from the crowd, reflecting wagers that had just been resolved. The fighters continued to bide their time. Billy landed a blow to Bones's stomach, and Bones responded in kind. Both punches appeared harder than the ones Bones had used to fell his opponents on the Fourth of July. Yet each man took the blow in stride.

Bones kept moving. When he didn't move, he got hit. Occasionally, Billy pushed his way inside, seeking to pummel Bones's body. When that happened, Bones grabbed at Billy's arms to smother his punching power.

Bones fired a right hand straight from the shoulder, putting his weight behind the blow. It landed on Billy Morris's cheek, and Billy went down.

For the first time, each fighter sat between rounds. "Time!"

I understood now that fighters were both born and made. Each man was possessed of extraordinary physical gifts and had studied his craft well. On occasion, one or the other risked his fists in the hope of landing a decisive blow to the skull. But by and large, they played a waiting game. It was hard to know who would benefit more from that strategy as the bout wore on. Meanwhile, Billy continued moving forward; applying pressure unceasingly with the agility of a man half his size.

The fourth round extended for twelve minutes, but the tension was such that the crowd stood riveted without any hint of complaint. Bones's jab landed regularly. Billy's face began to swell. Still, I presumed that Billy's punches were doing equal damage to Bones. Welts and bruises show more clearly on white skin than colored. Neither man fell deliberately to take a tactical rest. Both were traveling in a world where the margin for error was small.

The round ended when Billy landed a blow to Bones's body, and followed with a punch to the shoulder that put Bones down. Each man had now visited the turf twice. Bones had landed more blows, mostly with his jab. But Billy appeared the stronger of the two on some primitive level that I found hard to define.

"Time!"

A small stream of blood continued to trickle from

above Billy's eye. He advanced and Bones retreated in circular fashion. Both men's punches were now more ferocious than before. Yet there was not a wince or moan to confess the pain being inflicted upon them. Indeed, although I stood close by, I couldn't judge which blows told and which did not; they rained down like so many stones.

Then I realized that all blows told, though some told more than others. Billy scored with a horrible punch directly to Bones's ribs. Bones brought his elbows down to protect his body, and Billy launched another blow that landed on Bones's cheek. Then he returned to the body, striking as close as he could come to Bones's liver.

"Bones is hurt," Cowhand Bob told me in a voice that was barely audible.

Billy kept moving forward, fists pounding, anxious to make contact with any part of Bones's body.

Bones got hit ... got hit again ... staggered ... and fell.

I helped him to his feet and led him to the corner.

I'd never understood before what it meant to be a fighter. I'd assumed Bones would always be strong; that his endurance was inexhaustible. But the difference in size between the two men was simply too great, given their age and comparative skills. Billy wasn't just beating Bones. He was beginning to beat Bones up, badly.

"Time!"

Billy was throwing punches hard into Bones's body. The only hope Bones seemed to have lay above Billy's eye. The cut that had opened early in the fight was worsening. Stung by repeated jabs, it was now an inch-long crimson gash.

For the first time since the fight began, Bones spoke to his opponent.

"You're eye's bad, Billy. You're losin' blood."

Billy cracked Bones with another hard blow to the body. Just as quickly, Bones fired back with a right hand to the head. Very little that happened between them now was subtle. Both men fired a flurry of blows, and Bones went down.

The sun beat mercilessly through the haze. The air was hot and humid.

"Time!"

More blows. The pain caused by Billy's punches was becoming more and more evident. Bones spat out a tooth. His nose was bleeding. His forehead was swelling. He was holding on to survive. Billy knocked him down again, and raised his arms in triumph.

Cowhand Bob soaked a towel in water and draped it over Bones's head.

"Time!"

Bones lashed out with a right hand that fell short of the mark. Billy pressed forward, punishing him with thunderous blows to the body. Each blow was accompanied by a snort when thrown and a grunt of pain when it landed. A blow to the neck staggered Bones. Fighters hope to keep something in reserve to draw upon late in a fight. But Bones was using every ounce of strength he had simply to survive.

Billy knocked him down again.

"Time!"

The field of battle was red with blood. Bones now seemed defenseless.

Billy knocked him down once more.

"Time!"

Billy continued to score to the head and body, punching with abandon. Again, Bones fell to the ground; more this time from exhaustion than the force of Billy's blows.

Cowhand Bob and I dragged Bones to the corner. I looked at him and saw the battered face of a man who seemed to be dying.

"It's over," I said.

Bones looked at me uncomprehendingly.

"You're getting hurt. I'll do what I have to do. I'll beg, borrow, steal, anything, to get the money to keep you free. But you can't fight anymore. It's over."

When I was a boy, there were colored children who I considered friends of mine. But the truth is, the difference in our skins interposed a line that rendered true friendship impossible. In a test of wills, the colored side always had to yield. Thus, I was unprepared for what happened next.

Bones spat in my face.

"Shut your mouth, white boy."

"Bones—"

"Some little pussy put your pecker where your brains is, and now you're messing with my fight."

"Time!" the marshall said.

Within seconds, Bones was down again; the ninth time he'd been felled in the fight.

In the corner, I doused him with water.

Across the ring, Lamar Hughes held a bloody cloth to the cut above Billy's eye.

"Time!"

The entire right side of Bones's face was swollen, from the line of his jawbone to the top of his ear. Billy's face was far less marked, but his left eye was closing.

Billy moved forward, and Bones stepped back. I would not have looked had I known what was coming.

No, that is not true. My emotions were so powerful that they would have conquered all other feelings. In the excitement of the moment, I would have yielded and looked. Regardless, the instant that followed is now emblazoned in my mind. A fleeting moment of triumph and a nightmare that I cannot shake. An image that reminds me constantly of how contingent our lives are.

Billy readied himself to throw another thunderous blow. The type of punch he'd landed regularly throughout the fight. A blow with the force of a sledgehammer that would have further demolished Bones's body. Except, this one time only, Billy drew his left hand back a greater distance than proper in order to put extra force behind the blow. Thus, it took longer to deliver the punch than would otherwise have been the case.

And Bones struck to kill.

His right hand flashed and landed directly on Billy's

nose, shattering bone and spraying blood into the air. Only the strength of the muscles in Billy's legs kept him from collapsing. The look of a child, badly hurt, crossed Billy's eyes. And then, just as quickly as Bones had attacked—before I could rejoice—Billy struck back with a blow to the jaw that contorted Bones's face and sent him plummeting to the ground on the verge of unconsciousness.

Both men were now badly hurt, only in different ways. Billy Morris sat in his corner, slumped in pain. Bones was groggy, unable to command the movements of his own body. Each side worked feverishly in the thirty seconds allotted. Then—

"I'm talking to the fighters," Marshall Bassett said above the crowd. "I want everyone else, and particularly Mr. Clemens and Mr. Hughes, to keep their mouths shut."

The marshall gestured for Bones and Billy to advance to the center of the ring. Dark storm clouds had begun to gather. The air was heavy, almost unsupportable.

"Listen to me," the marshall said, addressing both fighters. "This has been a hard honest fight. Both of you are brave men, and both of you are hurting. Unless one of you objects, I'm declaring this fight a draw."

A draw. All bets would be off. But before I could complete the thought—

"No draw," Billy said.

"Time," the marshall ordered.

Bones still seemed confused from the blows he'd just endured. Both men threw punches, and he went down again.

Cowhand Bob and I helped Bones to the corner. As the thirty seconds passed, his eyes regained their focus and his mind began to clear.

"Time!"

More punches. Artistry and skill had now given way to courage. I was witnessing a spectacle that was savage and brutal, yet exhilirating at the same time. Both men pounded away, their knuckles raw and bleeding. Bones was exercising every ounce of strength in his battered body. Billy's shattered nose poured blood, and he gasped painfully for air. He had suffered more than a break. It was a horrifying wound. Both men were exhausted, yet both refused to yield.

Bones lashed out with a jab and followed with a hard right hand that landed flush on Billy's nose.

Billy's nose was grotesquely swollen. His face

resembled death. He looked less like a man than the nightmarish figment of a horror writer's imagination.

More blows, seemingly never ending.

Bones landed another right hand.

For the first time since early in the fight, Billy Morris went down.

In the corner, Cowhand Bob poured water on Bones.

Across the ring, Lamar Hughes worked feverishly with his fighter.

"Time!"

Bones was no longer fighting for freedom, and Billy was no longer fighting for money. They were fighting because neither man would submit to the will of the other. Each warrior was testing himself against every demon he'd known. The ring was hell for both men. But Bones had one advantage. An image of fire from childhood was seared in his mind. Unlike Billy Morris, Bones had been to hell before.

Bones landed his right hand again squarely on Billy's nose. There was an involuntary cry of pain .... Another blow .... And Billy crumbled to the ground.

A brooding oppressiveness hung in the air. The dark clouds and breathless heat seemed eerily foreboding.

Cowhand Bob took Bones by the arm and led him

to the corner. Lamar Hughes struggled to bring Billy to his feet, and sought to soothe his wounds with a full bucket of water.

I had dreamed of heroism before, but this was of a different order.

"Time!"

Lamar Hughes looked toward the marshall. Billy's other second put his hand over Billy's chest as though protecting Billy's heart. And then Hughes spoke the sweetest words I've ever heard.

"No more."

Relief and jubilation flooded into my heart.

Bones thrust his arms triumphantly in victory toward the sky.

There was shouting all around us, followed by a strange calm.

Then the sounds picked up again. A low murmur of discontent burgeoning into anger; flashing and crackling, spreading through the crowd.

"Get the nigger!"

The words were shouted loud and clear in a fiery Mississippi voice.

"Get the nigger!"

This time from another anonymous member of the

crowd.

I turned in one direction, then another, looking for help.

"Kill the nigger!"

And I knew they might .... I knew they might.

My eyes fixed on Marshall Bassett, who was looking at Bones.

"Get him out of here fast," the marshall ordered.

I grabbed Bones by the arm, and we began to run.

Lightning flashed. A deep peal of thunder rumbled through the sky.

Bones tripped and almost fell.

"Don't stop," I shouted.

Behind me, the marshall was trying desperately to still the crowd.

"Run," I urged. But Bones was hurting. His legs were unsteady, and it was hard for him to keep his body under control.

Then the storm let go.

A fierce flash of lightning revealed every blade of grass. A sweep of chilly air was followed by a deafening crash of thunder. The rain began to fall in sheets with unsurpassed might, thrashing the battered canyon walls.

"Satan is comin' to get someone," Bones cried in terror.

"Run!"

The drenching rain continued to pour amidst gusts of screaming wind. Another glare lit up the sky. Another furious roar. The elements blazed and boomed and raged with nature's full fury.

Bones stumbled and fell.

"Can't go no more," he cried.

A garish streak of lightning was followed by an ear-splitting thunderous blast.

Then, just ahead in the canyon wall, I saw the mouth of a cave. Dragging, pushing, pulling Bones with me, I made my way forward through nature's conflagration.

"Inside!" I shouted.

The storm was at its peak. Crashing, tearing, raging. But we had found sanctuary from both the elements and man.

We sat just inside the cave, gazing out at the slanting veil of rain. I hoped Cowhand Bob was safe, and told myself that the marshall would protect him. The small chamber at the mouth of the cave connected to a narrow passageway. After a while, with the rain still falling, I decided to explore our surroundings. Taking a lucifer match from my pocket, I moved toward the darkness. Then, when I could see no more, I scratched the match against my leg. Its tip lit, burned blue, and budded into a steady flame. Shielding the match with my hand, I continued forward. The passage was five feet wide and not much higher, with narrow crevices on either side. The match burned out, and I lit another before coming to a place where a thin stream trickled over a ledge into a pool of icy water. I thought of going further, but feared getting lost in a tangle of rifts and chasms; so I turned back and retreated to the mouth of the cave.

Bones was sitting still, staring out at the driving rain. His right eye was shut. Both of his hands were puffy, and it looked as though grapes had been inserted beneath the skin that covered his knuckles.

"I'm gettin' old," Bones said.

"You're only thirty-three."

"Thirty-three is old for fightin'. I got bruises deep all over my body, and my face don't feel good neither."

"You fought like a champion."

Bones allowed himself a smile. "I did some hurtin'; that's for sure. Both ways. I hurt him, and he hurt me.

But I give him credit; he fought like a man." Bones winced in pain. "Yes, sir; he fought like a man. I whupped him, but I give him credit. No throwin' was allowed, and he never throwed me. He never took unfair advantage; never broke the rules. Never done nothin' but look me in the eye and fight. Billy Morris is an honest fighter."

I led Bones to the dark place where the stream turned to a pool. He eased himself into the icy water and bathed his wounds in silence. After an hour, he rose up and we returned to the mouth of the cave. The rain had stopped. The sun was shining. But given the passions aroused by the fight, it seemed wise to wait until night before leaving.

Bones fell asleep. I sat beside him. I hoped that, this one time at least, he was dreaming.

Finally, darkness came.

I woke Bones, and we left the cave. It would be a long walk back to the ranch, but I calculated that we'd make it by midnight.

We began to walk. Bones was still hurting, but his legs were steady. There were no clouds in the sky, and stars were shining.

The way back to the ranch led past the spot where

the fight had been contested. Fifty yards from where the ring had been pitched, there stood a solitary tree. I hadn't noticed the tree before in the excitement of the drama.

I saw it now.

Hiram Kane was hanging from the tree. One end of a ring rope was tied around his neck. The other end extended to a branch pulled low by his weight. His body had been battered by stones now scattered in the dirt beneath his feet. His face was grotesquely distorted, bearing witness to the precise moment that life had been choked out of him. He was the deadest man I've ever seen.

Bones stared at the lifeless form and fell to his knees, sobbing.

I wanted to say something.

"He was a bad man," I offered at last, trying to provide a measure of comfort.

"It don't matter. People done awful things to make him the way he was. And whatever he was, the people that done this to him were worse."

CHAPTER 10

It was a long walk back to The Lazy Bird ranch, but Bones and I completed the journey by midnight. Cowhand Bob was safe in the bunkhouse. Hiram Kane was the only casualty of the day's events.

"It was the Mississippi boys that done him in," Cowhand Bob told us. "A lot of them lost money on the fight; and they was upset that Billy got beaten by a colored. When the lynching started, there was five hundred people there, and only two of them tried to stop it."

Marshall Bassett was one of the two.

The other was Billy Morris.

"But Billy was having trouble standing, let alone interfering with a mob," Cowhand Bob continued. "So the marshall was by himself. He did what he could, but it wasn't enough. And the sad thing is, out of those five hundred people, only a handful really wanted to do it. But the way folks is, if someone shouts, 'Lynch him,' there's others that join in because they don't want to look different. Then you have a hundred people screaming and yelling, and the rest are afraid to stand in their way."

On Monday, Bones and I went into town to collect the money owed to us. There was Lamar Hughes's thousand-dollar wager. And we were pleased to learn that five hundred and twelve people had paid a dollar each to watch the fight. Hughes had given the spectator money to Marshall Bassett for safekeeping, and the marshall passed it on to us. That meant Bones and I received one thousand five hundred and twelve dollars, which we converted into twenty-dollar gold pieces. I showed him how to sew his half into the lining of his shirt and pants, and we went to bed rich men on Monday night.

Fortunately, other than losing a tooth, Bones suffered no lasting injuries from the fight. The rest of his teeth had been loosened by blows; but once they settled, he was able to chew comfortably again. We stayed at The Lazy Bird for another week, and then I decided it was time to move on. I figured my fight-arranging days were over. And I was starting to think it would be nice to try my hand at riverboat piloting or some such other endeavor.

On Monday, the twenty-third of July, I said good-bye to Cowhand Bob. Then I went into town for the rest of my farewells. The owner of The Lazy Bird had suggested that Bones stay on as a cowhand at the ranch. But given his earnings from the fight, Bones thought he'd go north and eventually buy himself a piece of land, so he went into town with me.

The good-byes were difficult. The townfolk were good honest people, and they'd worked their way into my heart.

"Keep away from people who belittle your ambitions," Miss Lurleen told me, when I dropped by The Silver Slipper. "And never ever part with your dreams. You can be anything you want to be."

"You can't travel through life on another man's road, so stay your own course," the marshall advised me.

There remained the matter of Bones's freedom papers. This time, I got the formalities right. The marshall and the town banker witnessed the transfer. Then Marshall Bassett wrote out a letter, and read each word aloud to Bones.

"To whoever reads this. Mister Bones is under my

protection. He should be allowed to pass unmolested wherever his business takes him at any time. I request that Mister Bones always be given fair treatment as an honorable free man."

The marshall signed the letter with a flourish and handed it to Bones. "Going north is a good idea," he suggested. "North, and then maybe east. But at the start, point yourself toward the North Star."

I went outside to wait for the stagecoach. Bones came with me. I wasn't much for speeches at that time in my life, so I said simply, "Bones, I'm proud to know you."

"You're a good man," he told me.

I guess that was all the reward either of us needed, but I wanted to do something more. So I gave Bones one of my shirts; the one with the tobacco stain that hadn't come out and the tear on the back of the collar.

"There's five hundred dollars in the lining of this shirt. Don't lose it," I said.

Bones stared, almost uncomprehendingly.

I looked him straight in the eye. "It's yours. You earned it."

The stagecoach was coming into view. I extended my hand in a final act of friendship. Bones took it and, smiling through tears, wrapped his arms around me in as warm an embrace as I've ever had.

Then I went west. I thought I'd go back to visit the town some day, but I never did. You know how those things are. And while I've lived a lifetime since then, whenever I think of the summer of 1856, the years seem to fade away. The ink with which history is written is merely fluid prejudice. But I've tried to recount those six weeks as fairly and honestly as possible. Many of the people I've spoken about are now in Heaven. Some, I trust, are in the other place. But all the faces are as clear in my thoughts as they were fifty-four years ago, including mine.

Eventually, I did in fact become a riverboat pilot. The truth is, when I was a boy, there was but one permanent ambition among my comrades in Hannibal, and that was to be a steamboatman. We had transient ambitions of other sorts. When a circus came to town, it left us all burning to be clowns. The first minstrel show to come our way infused in us the desire to try that kind of life. On occasion, we even hoped that God would permit us to be pirates. But those ambitions faded quickly, and the ambition to be a steamboatman remained.

In April of 1857, I began to apprentice as a pilot. In due course, I got my license, and the waters of the Mississippi became a wonderful book delivering to me their most cherished secrets. Time drifted smoothly, and I thought I'd follow the river for the rest of my life. However, the Civil War intervened and commerce on the Mississippi was suspended. In search of a new livelihood, I traveled west to Nevada with my brother Orion, who had been appointed secretary to the governor of Nevada. Thereafter, I served in quick succession as a silver miner and a newspaper reporter in Nevada, a gold miner and a newspaper reporter in California, and a special correspondent to the Sandwich Islands.

On the second day of October 1866, I gave my first lecture before a paying audience at the Academy of Music in San Francisco. The subject was travel; my remarks were well-received; and I found myself with an enthusiastic following. The next year, I journeyed to Europe and the Holy Land as a correspondent for a San Francisco newspaper. Then my first book, *The Innocents Abroad*, was published. To my delight, it sold one hundred thousand copies and gave me a literary reputation, which is how I stumbled into authorship as a career without intending it.

In 1870, at age thirty-four, I married Miss Olivia Langdon. My beloved Livy was gentle and divinely good, with a sweetness and serenity in her face that reflected her spiritual nature. Livy was the only sweetheart I ever truly loved. Her father, a wealthy coal baron from upstate New York, disapproved of me at first but eventually consented to our marriage. We lived briefly in Buffalo, and then moved to a mansion in Hartford. For the rest of my life, Livy was sacred to me. Not every day is a sunshine day. The human condition simply isn't that way. But whatever amount of sunshine would otherwise have existed in my life, there was more because of Livy.

After Livy and I wed, good fortune continued to pour down upon me. My success as a scribbler of books continued. More people than I could have hoped for, or dreamed of, paid to hear me lecture. I began to associate with scholars and artists, and then with presidents and kings.

In 1887, my status as a celebrity brought me to Chicago. I was fifty-two years old by then, and had grown accustomed to the trappings of fame. The purpose of my visit was to lecture on politics, and I was rather pleased with my performance.

I began with a touch of cynicism: "The chances are that a man cannot get elected to Congress without resorting to tactics that render him unfit to be there." I moved next to humor; and after that, to sentimentality. Ninety minutes after beginning, I closed with the thought, "True patriotism, the only rational patriotism, is loyalty to the nation all the time, loyalty to the government when it deserves it."

Then, after the customary ovation, I gathered my notes and prepared to leave the stage, when I saw a woman of elegant carriage making her way down the aisle toward me. She looked to be about sixty years of age. And while my normal instinct under those circumstances is to cringe, knowing that I'm about to be subjected to tedious compliments or unwanted debate, something about her led me to welcome her approach.

"Sam?"

And in that moment, I was twenty years old again.

"Hello, Lurleen."

We embraced before stepping back to gaze fondly upon one another. It took a moment for me to accept the fact that, while I'd been growing older, Miss Lurleen hadn't been standing still in that matter. But she was still a wonderful-looking woman, with a

warmth and joy in her face that I hadn't fully appreci-
ated when I was young. She told me of her life since
Kansas; how she'd moved to Chicago in 1866 to open a
finer establishment; that she'd never married, but had
lived for years with a woman friend, which I thought I
understood. Then she told me about some of the other
townfolk, and I uttered names that had been silent
upon my lips for decades as though they were music.

Marshall Bassett had kept his job for fifteen more
years before retiring. He was still in good health at age
sixty-five, and exchanged letters regularly with
Lurleen.

Cowhand Bob was married with children and
grandchildren, and owned a small ranch.

Pete had fallen down a well and drowned.

Mona married a cowhand from The Lazy Bird, and
they'd moved to a neighboring community where she
wasn't quite as well-known.

Judith had taken over management of The Silver
Slipper when Lurleen left for Chicago. "She's a smart
woman," Lurleen told me. "She runs the place just
fine."

I didn't ask about Nell. Part of me hoped Lurleen
would mention her name, and part of me hoped she

wouldn't. Finally, near the end of our conversation, Lurleen volunteered, "After Mona got married, Nell came to the saloon, asking for a job. I told her no. I like my women honest. Not long after that, she sold what was left of her farm and moved on." Responding to the look in my eyes, Lurleen softened her voice. "Sam; Nell was never anything like what you thought her to be. You gave her credit for being a far better person than she was."

Then Lurleen asked what had become of Bones.

I didn't know.

In the mid-1800s, a man could easily disappear in the United States. There had been no place where Bones and I could write to each other. And even if there had been, he couldn't read or write.

In my fantasies, Bones is a happy man. He has taken the money he won against Billy Morris, bought some land, and lived a long productive life. But I know it's equally possible, if not likely, that he was swindled of his fortune and forced by necessity to enter the ring again. Perhaps it's better for my own peace of mind that he disappeared without a trace. Still, I think of him often.

I said earlier in this narrative that, to arrive at a just

estimate of a man's character, one must judge him by the standards of his time. But judged by the standards of any era, Bones was remarkable. His character was replete with qualities that engender respect, and his soul was fashioned from truth. If freedom is loyalty to one's best self, then Bones was truly free. He experienced bitter griefs and horrifying assaults in his life, but never allowed them to sour his spirit.

I've come in contact with many exceptional people during my days. I've exchanged ideas with Charles Darwin, and discussed literature with Robert Browning, Lewis Carroll, Henry James, Rudyard Kipling, and Robert Louis Stevenson. I've been privileged to meet three Presidents of the United States, King Edward VII of England, Emperor William II of Germany, and a King of Sweden whose name I forget. Yet none of these luminaries was more remarkable than Bones. And his character shines even more brightly when I consider the brutalization that he endured.

I believe that slavery is mankind's greatest crime. It is simply not possible for anyone of humanity and intelligence to construct a rational defense of slavery. There can be no justification for consigning millions of men and women at birth to a lifetime of imprisonment without any wrongdoing of their own. Yet Bones transcended all of that, and his memory has served me well these many years. No courage is absolutely perfect, but his came close. He was a better man than I was, although he gave scant evidence of knowing it. I am privileged to have lived in his world.

Even now, in quiet moments, I close my eyes and see Bones. It is a curious thing; this space-annihilating power of thought. For a while now, I've been floating through Kansas, revisiting images from a half-century ago. In many ways, I was an ignorant young man then. And I suppose I'm an ignorant old man now. But so much has happened since that time .... The Civil War which, like all wars, involved the killing of strangers against whom there was no personal animus .... The assassination of President Lincoln; the most horrific act in the history of the republic .... And the rise of a class of men—robber barons, if you will—who act as though they have not a shadow of a notion of the difference between good and evil.

The way of life I knew as a child has been supplanted by the establishment of great fortunes. The gospel of getting rich by any means has rotted the fruit of the American Revolution. Robber barons have elevated the worship of wealth in this country beyond all other values. They've seized control of the government and corrupted public morals. And despite their fabulous lucre, the rich don't care for anybody but themselves. It's only the poor who have feeling for the poor and try to help the downtrodden.

My own fortunes have fared poorly in this era of ruthless entrepreneurial skills. When I was young, most everything I touched turned to gold. But lately, there has been a profusion of coal. I founded a publishing firm, but after flaring brilliantly, it failed. Then I purchased all rights to a typesetting machine that I thought would become the literary equivalent of the cotton gin. That venture cost Livy and myself every dollar we had and virtually every possession we owned. At age sixty, to avoid the stigma of bankruptcy, I was forced to sell our home and embark upon a round-the-world lecture tour.

I've lived in the twentieth century for about ten years now, and I don't like the start of this century any more than the end of the last one. There's a new invention called the automobile, which will transform the way people travel; and another invention called the aeroplane, which won't make a bit of difference because no one will want to travel through the air when they can get from one place to another faster and more safely with the assistance of a horse.

And in this century, I've experienced death, too grievously and far too often. Livy and I had four children together. Langdon, our first child and only son, died many years ago at the age of two. The doctors said it was diphtheria, but I believe pneumonia also played a role. Then we lost Susy. She was a physically delicate child, who exhibited sensitivity and understanding towards others at an unusually early age. Susy died of spinal meningitis when she was twenty-four, as Livy and I were returning to the United States from my global lecture tour.

Then came the most crushing blow. When Livy was sixteen, she had fallen on ice and been injured in a way that left her partially paralyzed and unable to walk. She recovered from that condition, but suffered from a series of physical ailments and melancholia throughout her life. After Susy's death, Livy's health further declined. The gaiety vanished from her face, and she was prone to long periods of nervous prostration. In 1902, she began to have trouble breathing and was confined to bed. Two years later, she died.

MARK TWAIN REMEMBERS

It was my prayer that Livy and I should pass from this world together. But she is gone now, and I endure. Old habits die hard. When I wake in the night and rise from bed, I creep in a tiptoe so as not to disturb her. Then I'm reminded by the empty bed that I cannot disturb her anymore. I should like to have Livy's head on my shoulder again. Life without her is not life as I knew it before.

After Livy's death, the Clemens family virtually ceased to exist, but there was one more loss to endure. Jean, my youngest daughter, was blessed with a wit like my own. Epilepsy was her curse. She suffered from it throughout her life. Last Christmas Eve, a final attack took her from this world.

That leaves me only with Clara; my third-born child and last surviving seed. Like her mother, Clara has suffered from nervous symptoms that render her indisposed for long periods of time. Now she has married a Jew and gone away to live in Europe. How poor am I, who was once so rich. There are graves where once I enjoyed firesides.

Meanwhile, all this dying has got me contemplating my own death. And when an old man is facing death, he thinks a lot about God.

I believe in God the Almighty. I do not believe in the Biblical presentation of God. It contradicts my reason. I do not believe God has ever sent a message to man by anybody, or made Himself visible to mortal eyes in any place at any time. I believe that the Old and New Testaments and all the other sacred texts of the world were imagined and written by man, and that no line in them was authorized by God.

The God of the Bible is a contradictory master. He preaches mercy, yet invented hell. One day, he coaxes and pets a handful of nomads. The next day, he harries and lashes out at them. He punishes innocent children for the misdeeds of their parents, and wreaks vengeance upon unoffending populations for the wrongdoing of their rulers. Not even dumb cattle are safe from his wrath.

We are told that not a sparrow falls to the ground without the God of the Bible seeing it; yet it falls just the same. He restores sight to blind men now and then, but never to all the blind. He cures a cripple, but never all cripples. The God of the Bible, we are told, could extinguish all suffering in a moment if he chose. So why does he not do so? Even poor ungodlike man takes responsibility for the welfare of his own children. Is it too much to ask the same of God?

But consider, if you will, the true Creator; a God as vast as everything; a God of awesome majesty and grandeur; the One who created this majestic universe and rules it. He is the only Originator; the perfect artisan. He is not jealous or petty or vindictive. He cares nothing for man's flatteries; it is impossible that he should listen to them. His character is written in His real Bible, which is Nature and nature's history. Nature is a God whose constant ordering of the universe is steadfast in purpose, impartial, and fair.

I have even dreamed that the entire natural universe is the colossal physical person of God; that the vast worlds we see twinkling millions of miles apart are the blood corpuscles in His veins; that we, like all other living creatures, are the microbes that charge His corpuscles with life. This, to me, has far more truth in it than to believe the Creator intentionally made man, has a passion for man, and listens to man. We are not as important as we suppose we are.

Yet it is a privilege to be alive. At first, I couldn't understand what I was made for. Then I came to know that certain rights and responsibilities accompany living. Now I believe that I was put here to search out the secrets of this world and to thank the Giver of it all for devising everything. True prayer, to my mind, is a moment of reflection about oneself. Am I doing all that I can do to become a better person? Am I using this precious gift of life in a way that justifies what the Creator has given me? At some point soon, I shall cease to exist in the world of time and space that we know. I pray that, when all is done, I will have been faithful to my Creator.

Meanwhile, I can't hurry this dying business. At times, I've thought of trying. Age is upon me with the indignity of its infirmities, and I'm like an old burnt-out crater. They keep trying to confer this honorary degree upon me and that honorary degree upon me, and I don't want them. I'm tired of all the banquets and dinners, and I am resolved not to go to any more; not even The Last Supper. Most everyone I've loved is dead and gone. My dreams have vanished; and when dreams are gone, one might still exist but one has ceased to live. Sometimes I wonder if there isn't something I can simply resign to be out of it all.

When I seem to be dying, I don't want to be stimulated back to life. All I want is to be made comfortable to go. Then I shall step aboard my waiting ship and lay my course with a reconciled spirit and contented heart toward the setting sun. And in time, I shall arrive at that place where everything is pitch black and each little pinprick of light seems like an exploding star.

Death, that kindly friend who brings peace and healing to all, is upon me. I shall soon be silent.